EEK & ACK

BEYOND THE BLACK HOLE

Librarian Reviewer
Katharine Kan
Graphic novel reviewer and Library Consultant, Panama City, FL
MLS in Library and Information Studies, University of Hawaii at
Manoa, HI

Reading Consultant
Elizabeth Stedem
Educator/Consultant, Colorado Springs, CO
MA in Elementary Education, University of Denver, CO

STONE ARCH BOOKS
www.stonearchbooks.com

Graphic Sparks are published by Stone Arch Books
151 Good Counsel Drive, P.O. Box 669
Mankato, Minnesota 56002
www.stonearchbooks.com

Library of Congress Cataloging-in-Publication Data
Hoena, Blake A.
Beyond the Black Hole / by Blake A. Hoena; illustrated by Steve Harpster.
p. cm. — (Graphic Sparks. Eek and Ack)
ISBN 978-1-4342-0759-3 (library binding : alk. paper)
ISBN 978-1-4342-0855-2 (pbk. : alk. paper)
1. Graphic novels. [1. Graphic novels. 2. Science fiction.] I. Harpster, Steve, ill. II. Title.
PZ7.7.H64Bey 2009
[Fic]—dc22 2008006709

Summary: While zipping through space in their rocket-powered washing machine, Eek and Ack get sucked into a black hole. Moments later, they're spit out on the other side of space. The new universe has its own planet Earth, but it's a weird pink color. Of course, that won't stop this terrible twosome from trying to conquer it.

Art Director: Heather Kindseth
Graphic Designer: Brann Garvey

Printed in the United States of America

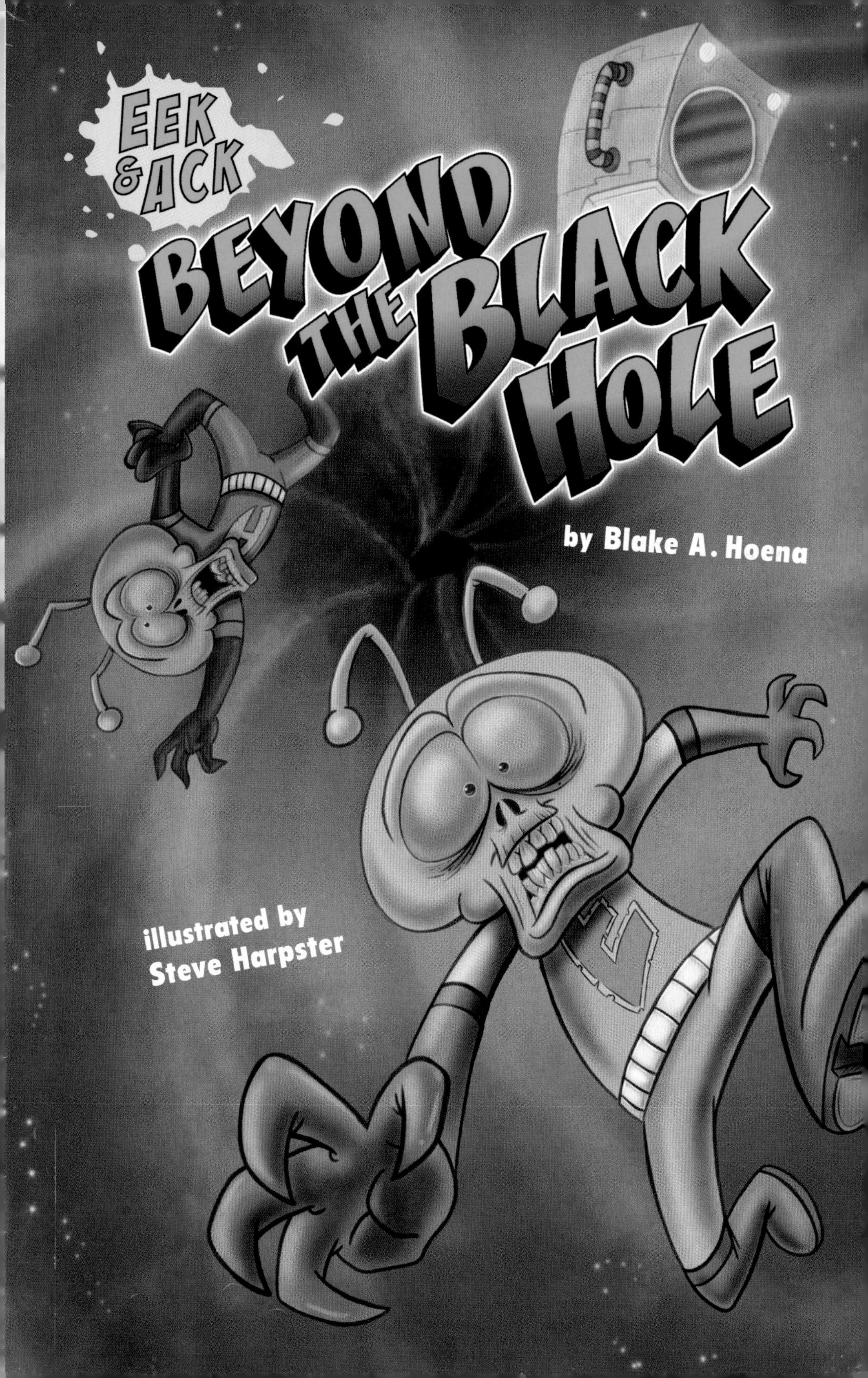
EEK & ACK
BEYOND THE BLACK HOLE
by Blake A. Hoena
illustrated by
Steve Harpster

CAST OF CHARACTERS

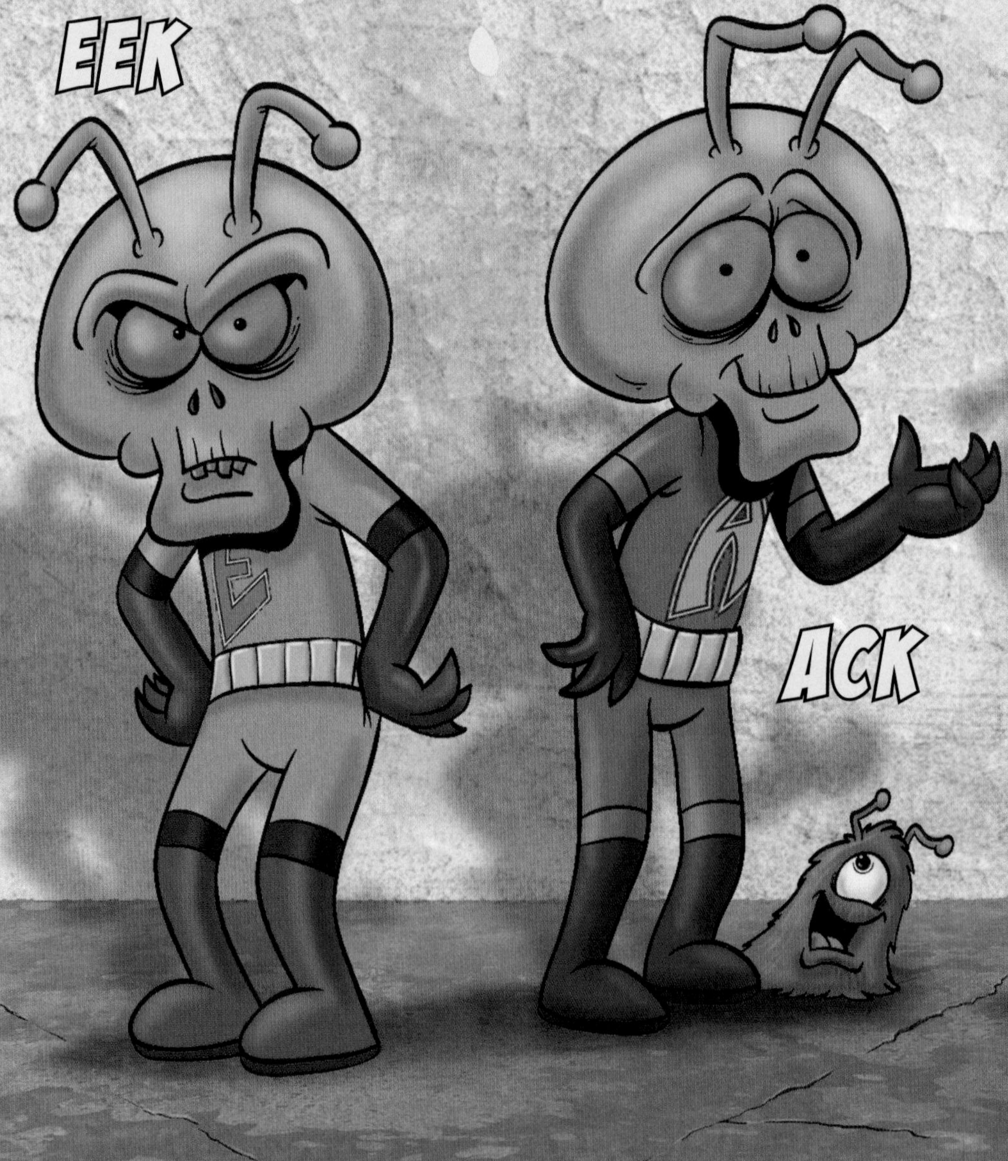
EEK
ACK

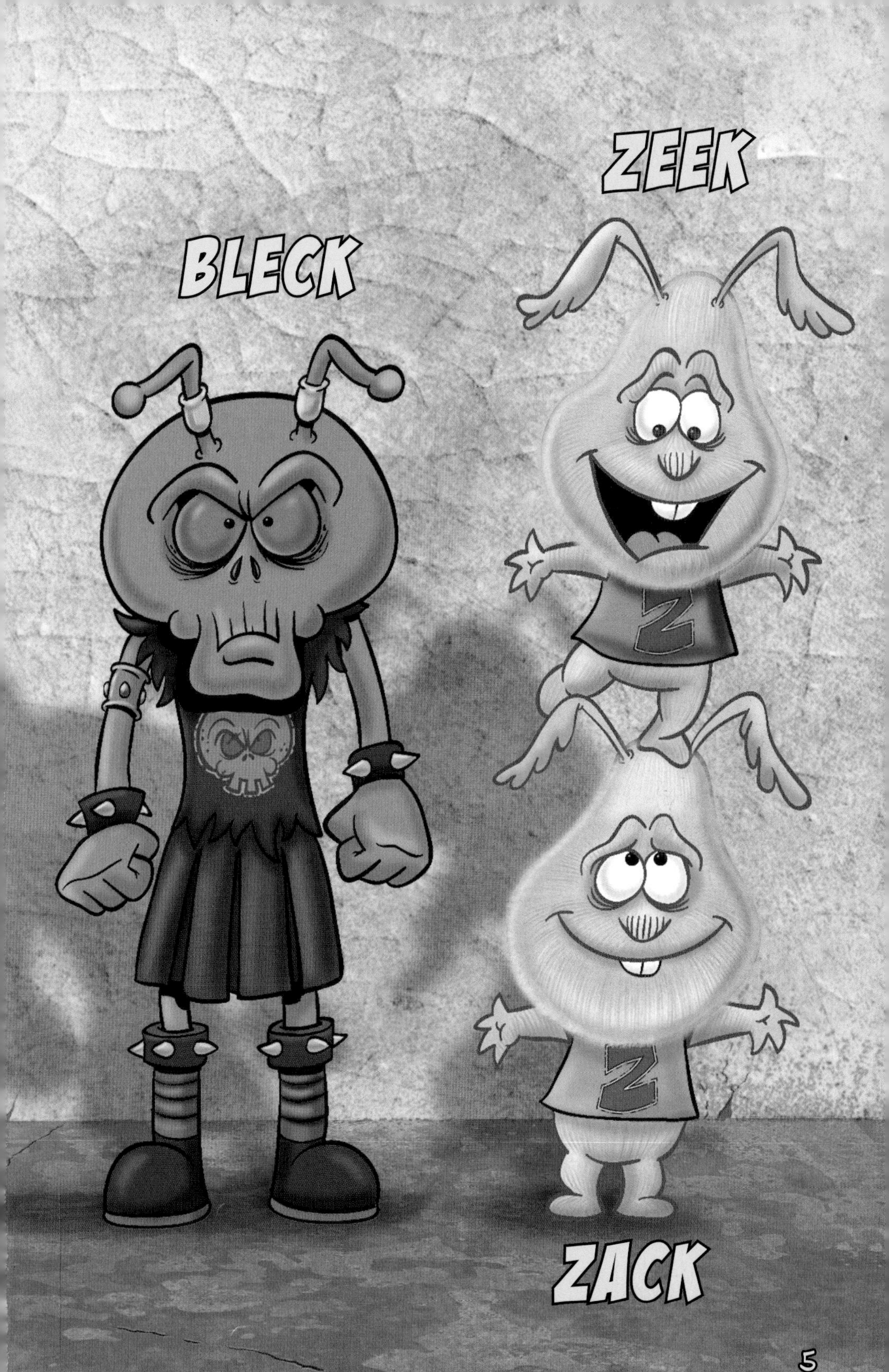
ZEEK
BLECK
ZACK

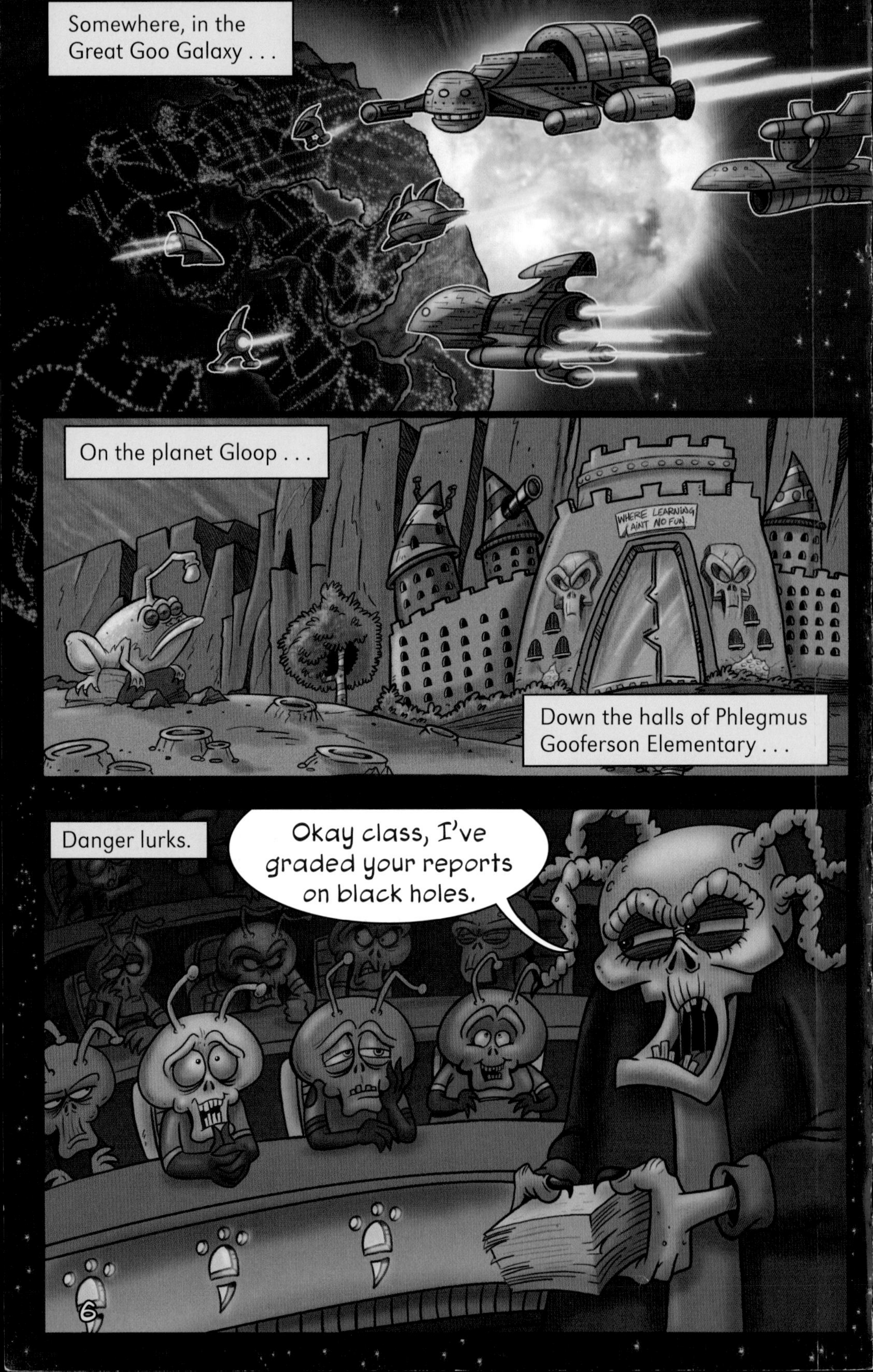
Somewhere, in the Great Goo Galaxy . . .
On the planet Gloop . . .
WHERE LEARNING AINT NO FUN
Down the halls of Phlegmus Gooferson Elementary . . .
Danger lurks.
Okay class, I've graded your reports on black holes.

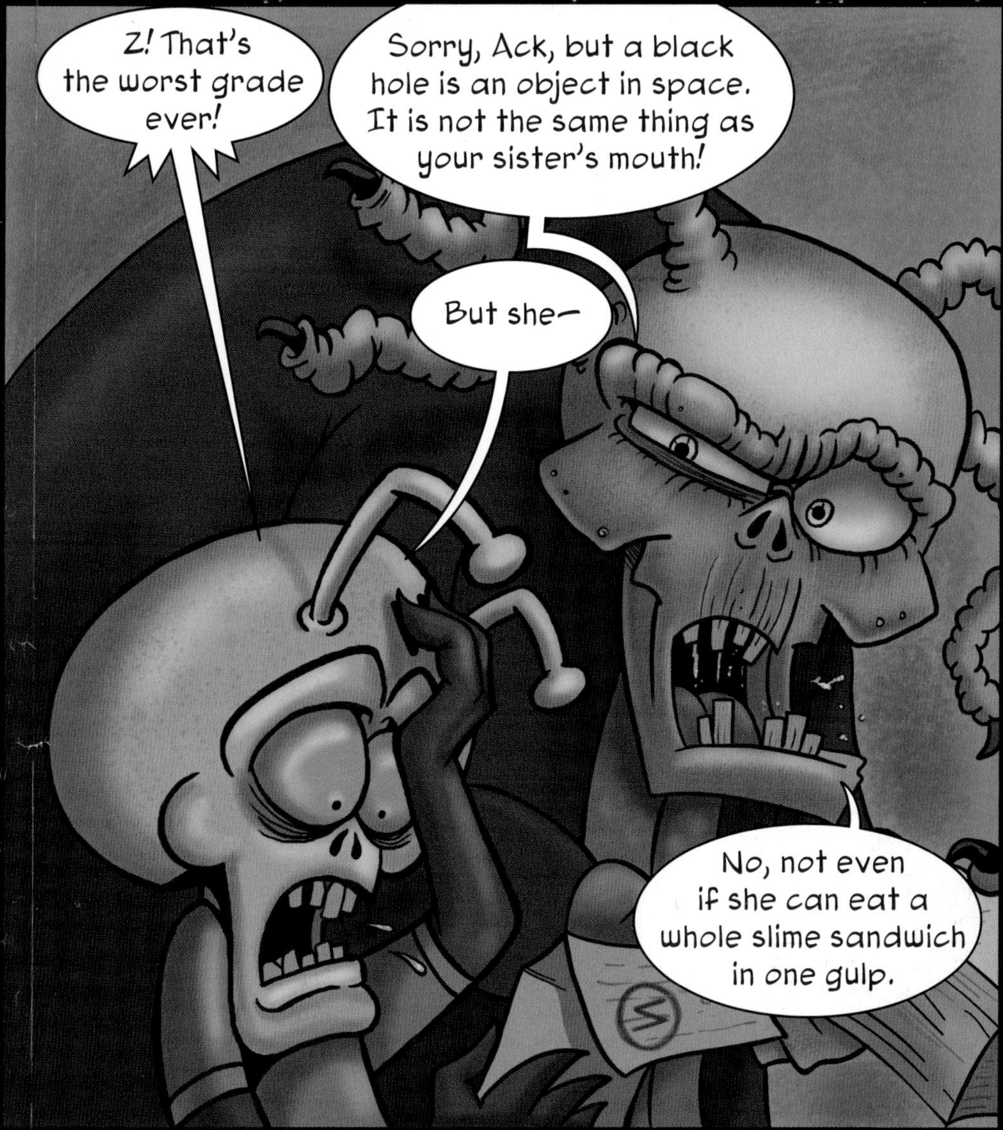
Z! That's the worst grade ever!
Sorry, Ack, but a black hole is an object in space. It is not the same thing as your sister's mouth!
But she—
No, not even if she can eat a whole slime sandwich in one gulp.

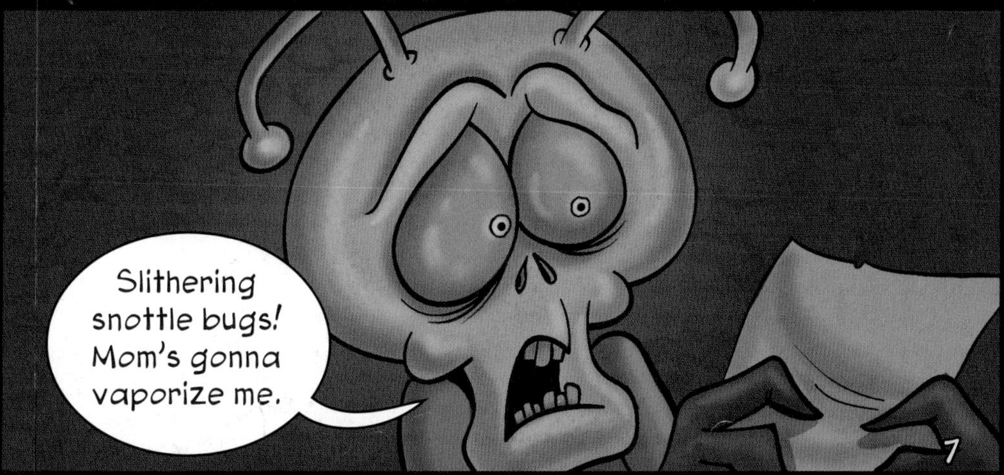
Slithering snottle bugs! Mom's gonna vaporize me.

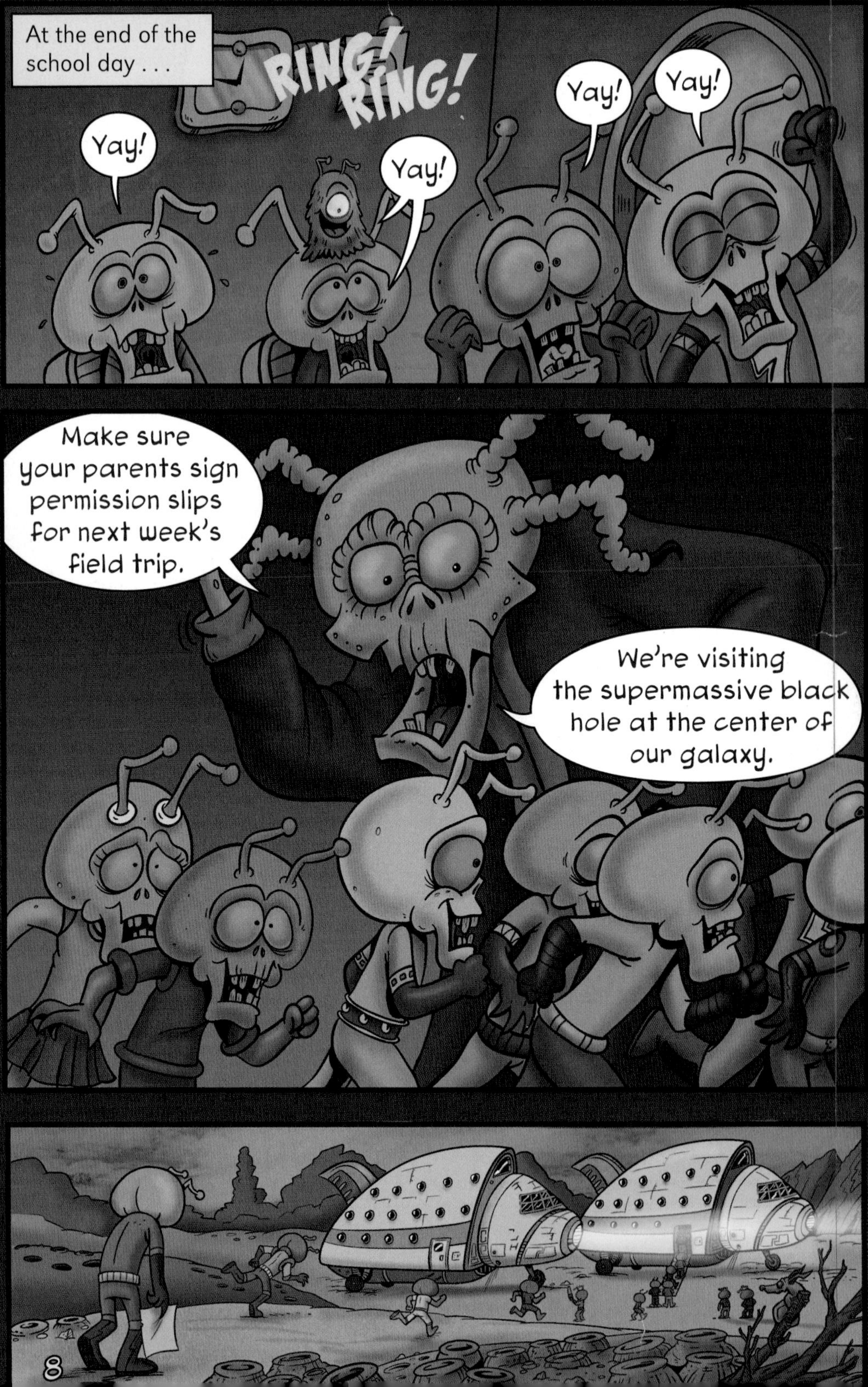
At the end of the school day . . .
RING! RING!
Yay!
Yay!
Yay!
Yay!
Make sure your parents sign permission slips for next week's field trip.
We're visiting the supermassive black hole at the center of our galaxy.

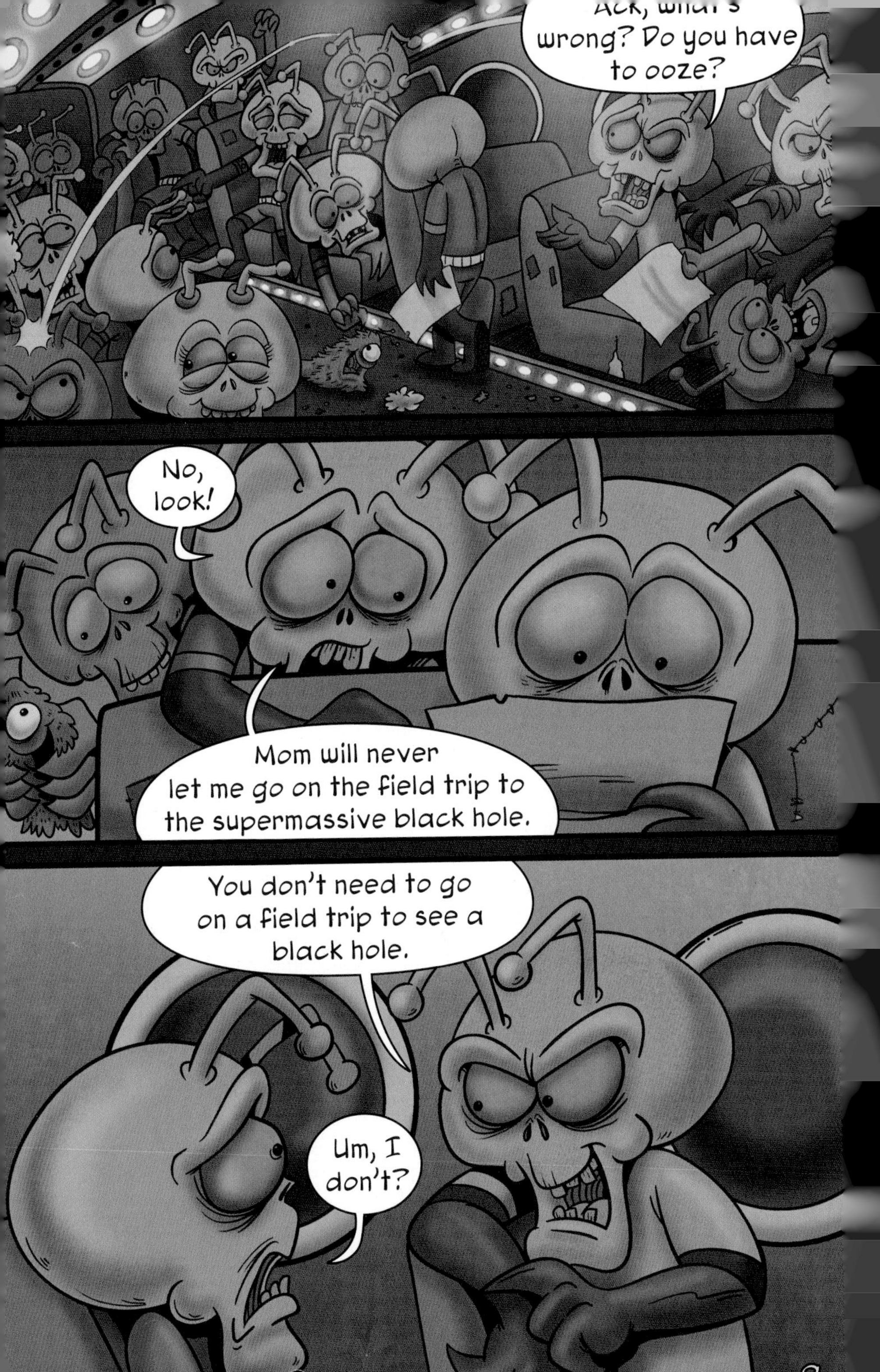
wrong? Do you have to ooze?
No, look!
Mom will never let me go on the field trip to the supermassive black hole.
You don't need to go on a field trip to see a black hole.
Um, I don't?

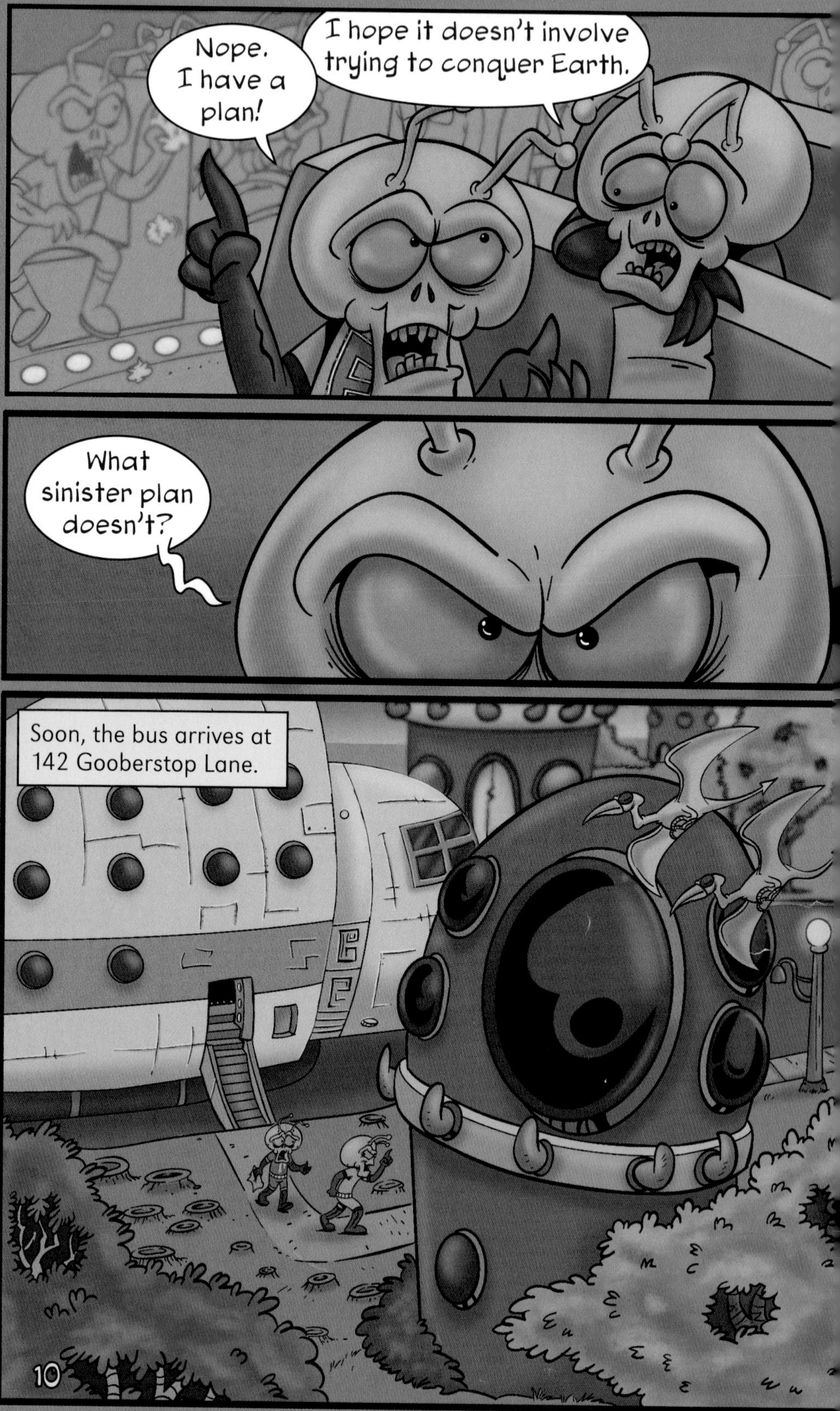
Nope. I have a plan!
I hope it doesn't involve trying to conquer Earth.
What sinister plan doesn't?
Soon, the bus arrives at 142 Gooberstop Lane.

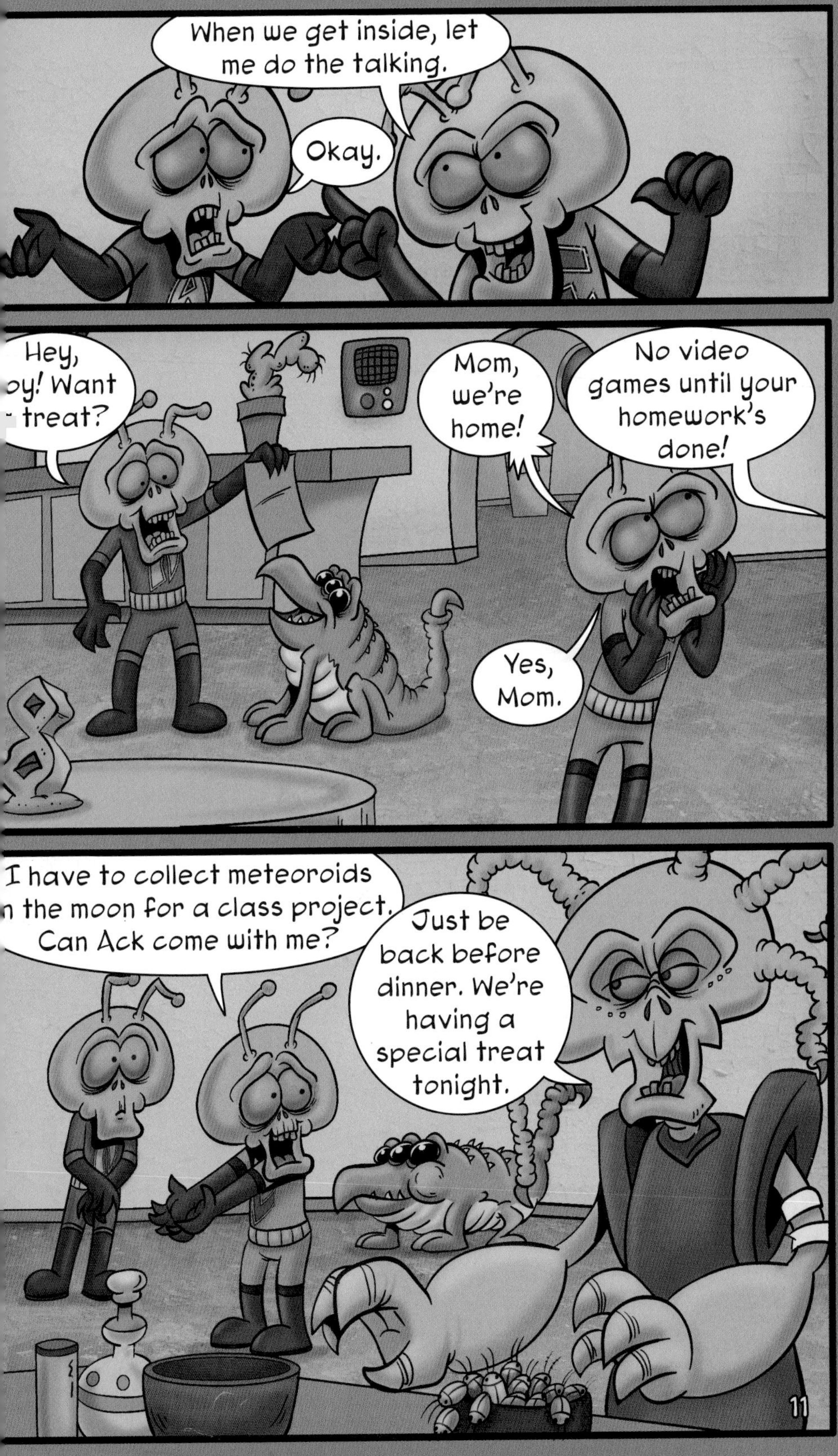
When we get inside, let me do the talking.
Okay.
Hey,
oy! Want
treat?
Mom, we're home!
No video games until your homework's done!
Yes, Mom.
I have to collect meteoroids
n the moon for a class project.
Can Ack come with me?
Just be back before dinner. We're having a special treat tonight.

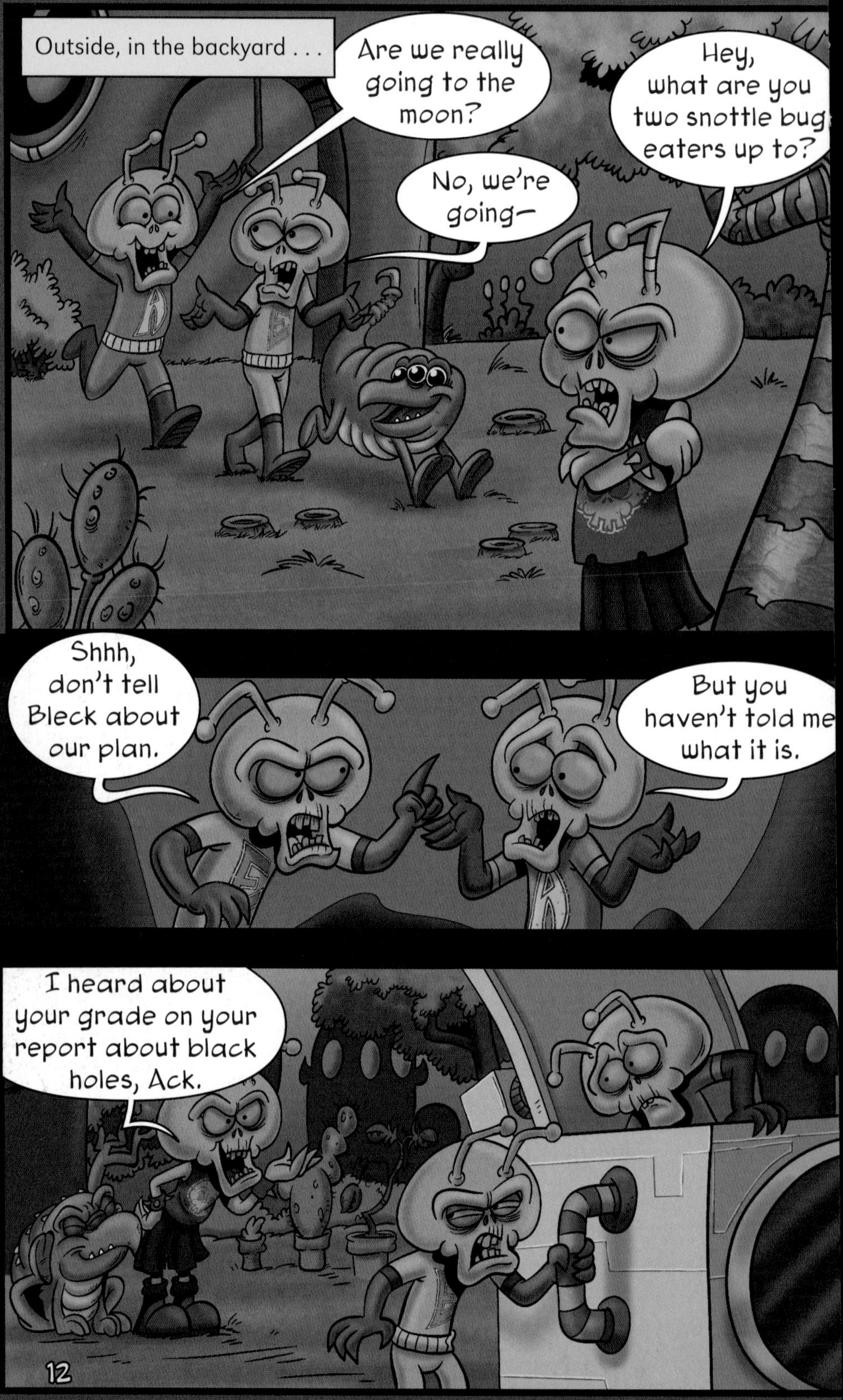
Outside, in the backyard . . .
Are we really going to the moon?
No, we're going—
Hey, what are you two snottle bug eaters up to?
Shhh, don't tell Bleck about our plan.
But you haven't told me what it is.
I heard about your grade on your report about black holes, Ack.
12

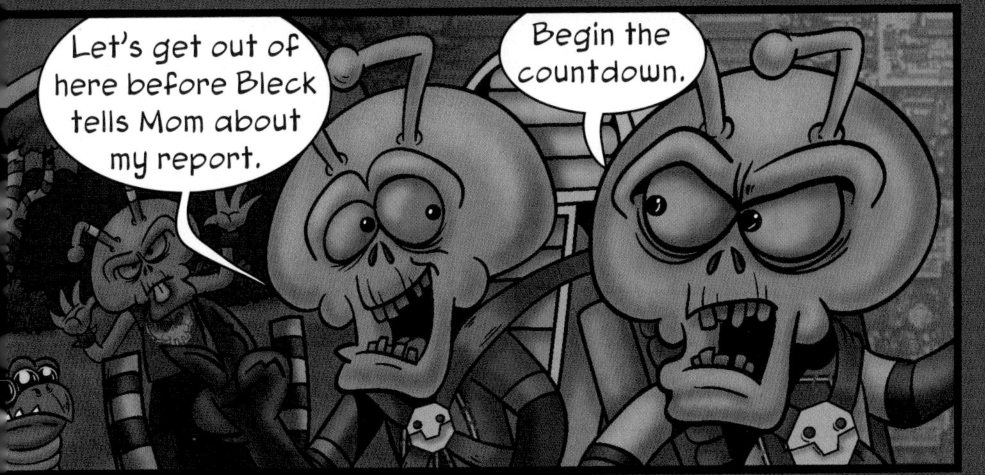
Let's get out of here before Bleck tells Mom about my report.
Begin the countdown.

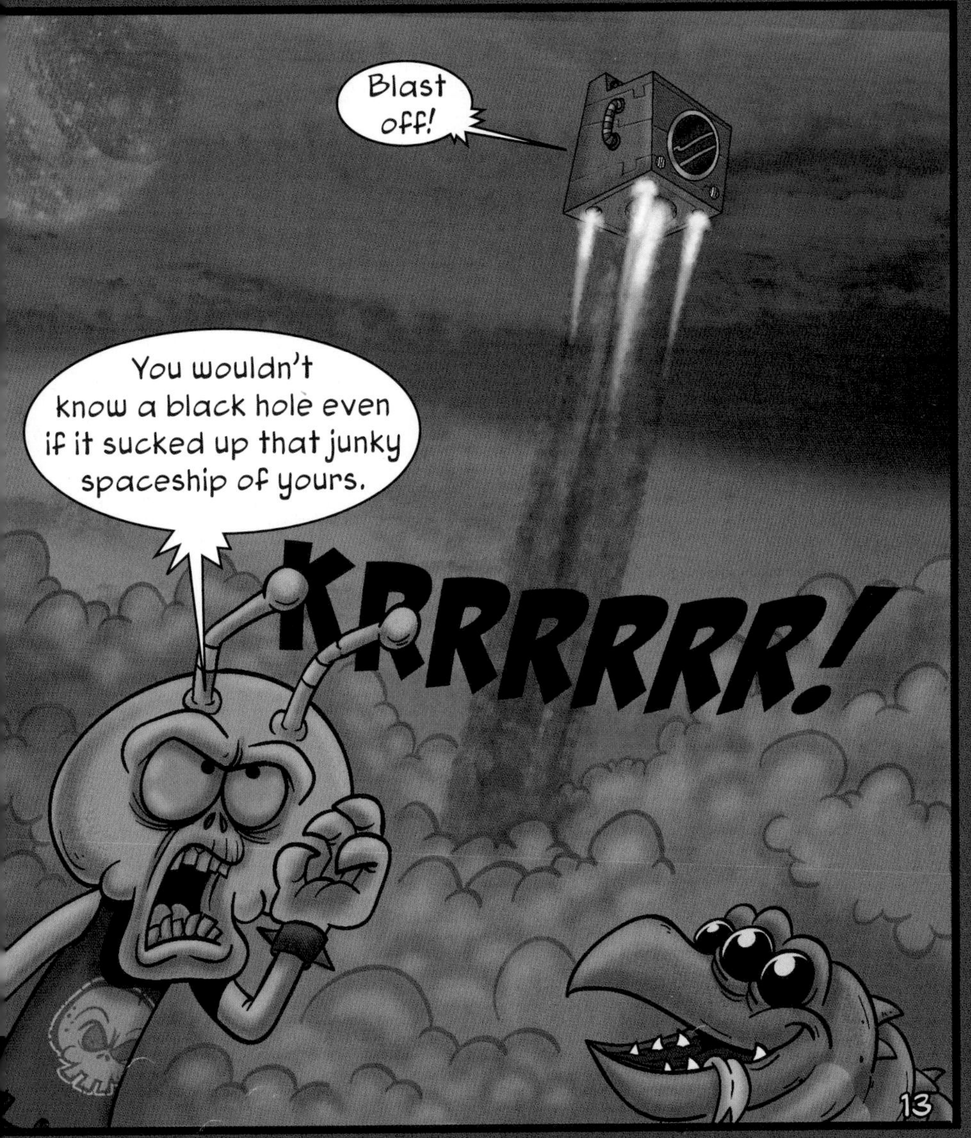
Blast off!
You wouldn't know a black hole even if it sucked up that junky spaceship of yours.
KRRRRRR!

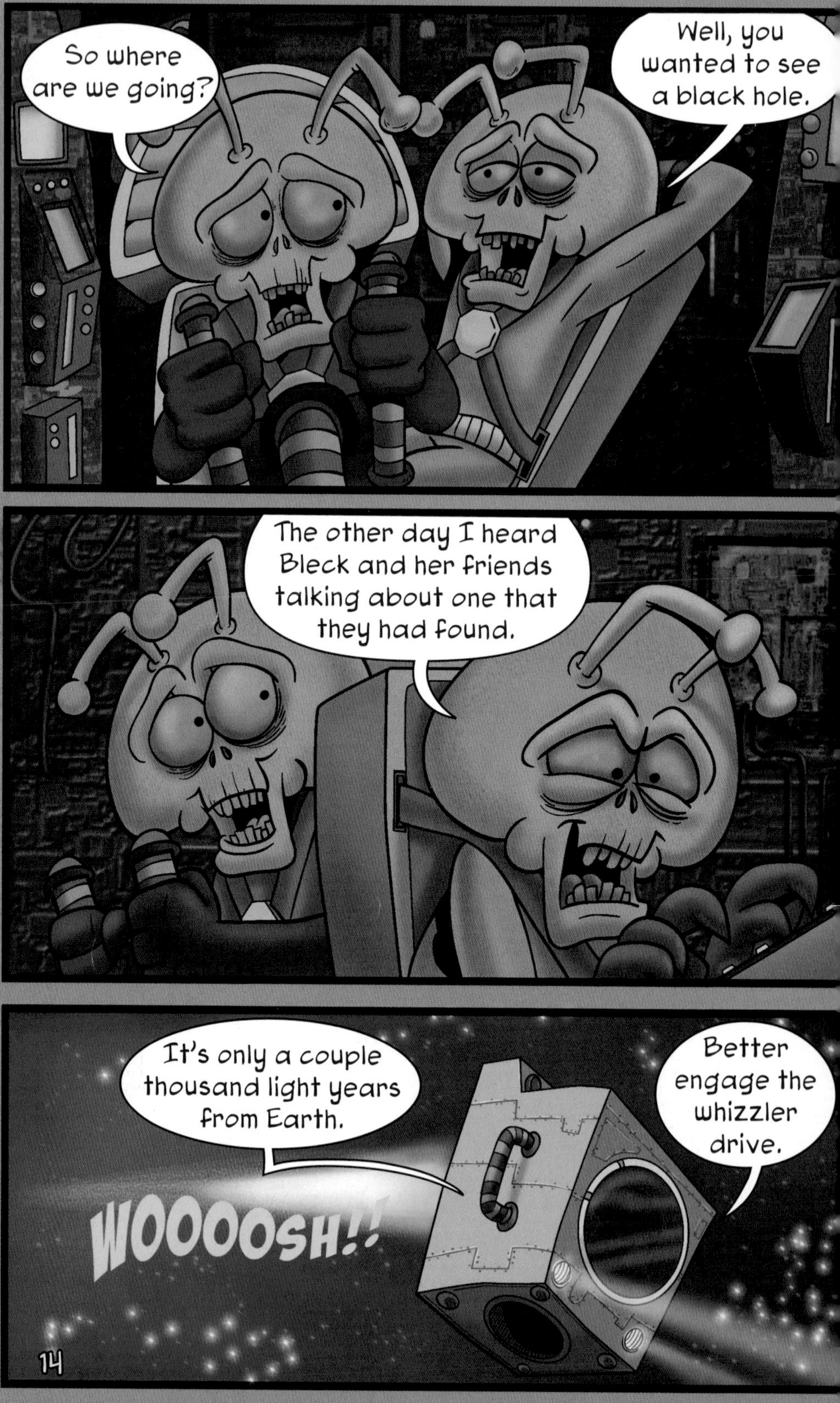
So where are we going?
Well, you wanted to see a black hole.
The other day I heard Bleck and her friends talking about one that they had found.
It's only a couple thousand light years from Earth.
Better engage the whizzler drive.
WOOOOSH!!

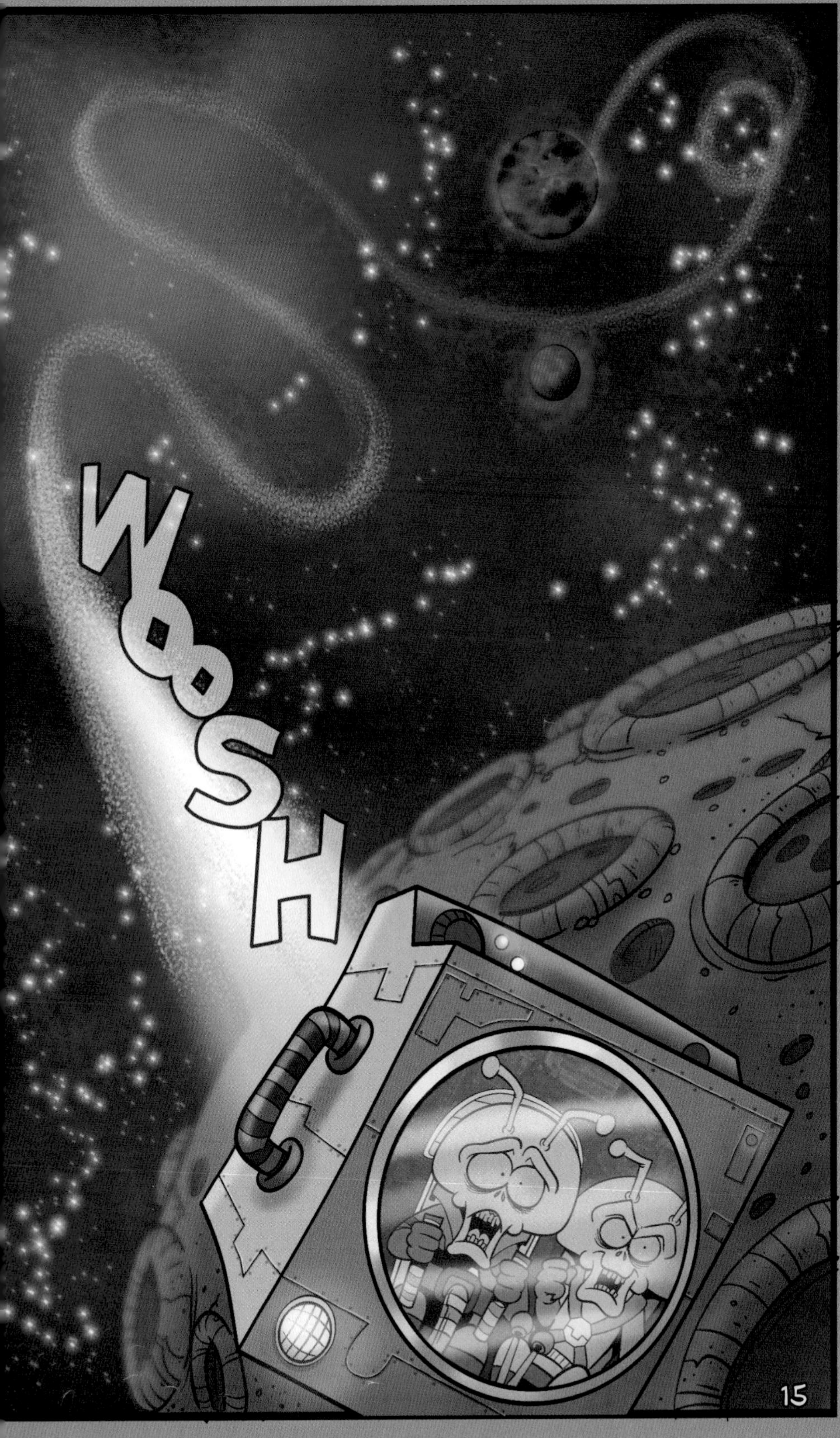
WOOSH

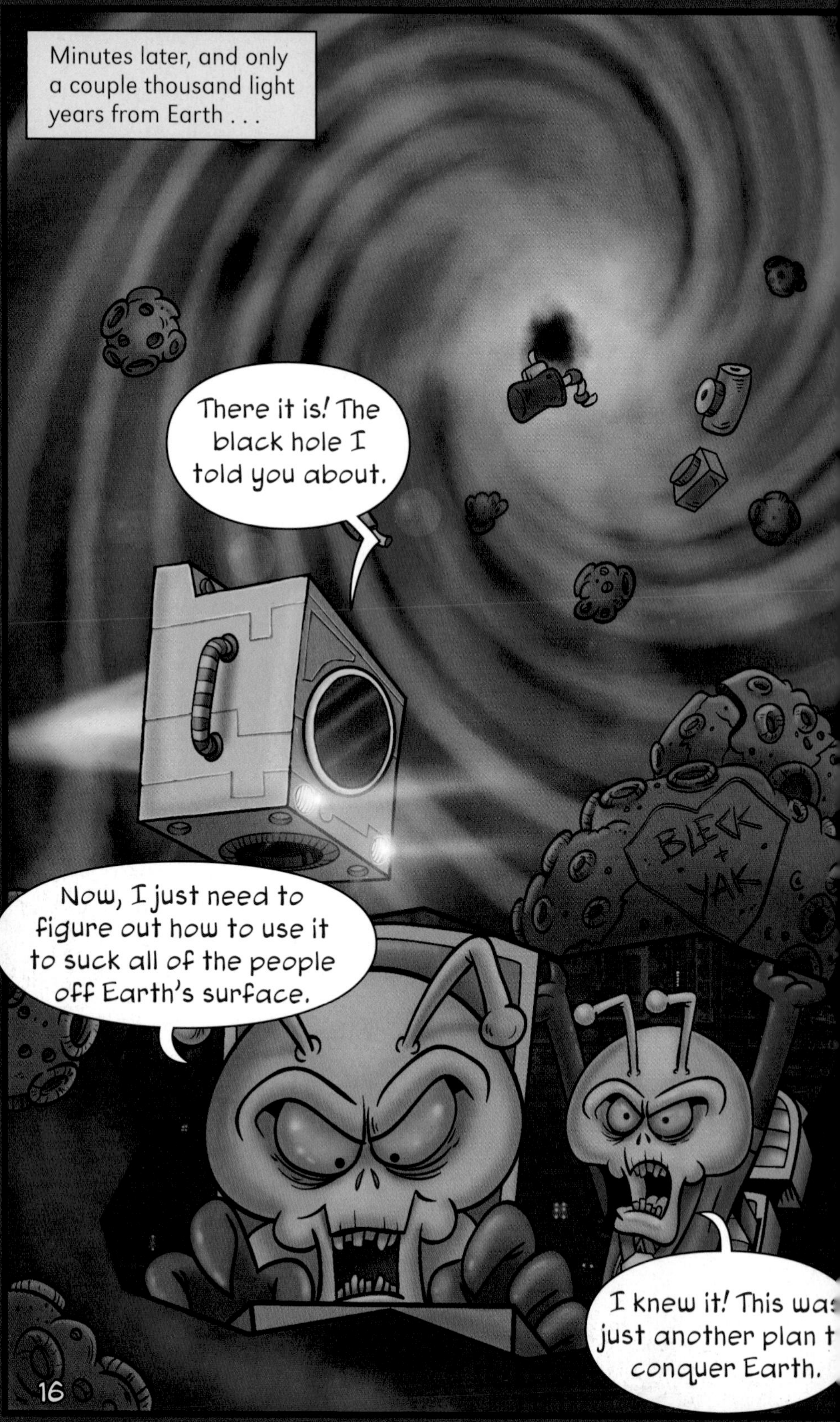

Minutes later, and only a couple thousand light years from Earth . . .
There it is! The black hole I told you about.
Now, I just need to figure out how to use it to suck all of the people off Earth's surface.
I knew it! This wa just another plan t conquer Earth.
BLECK + YAK

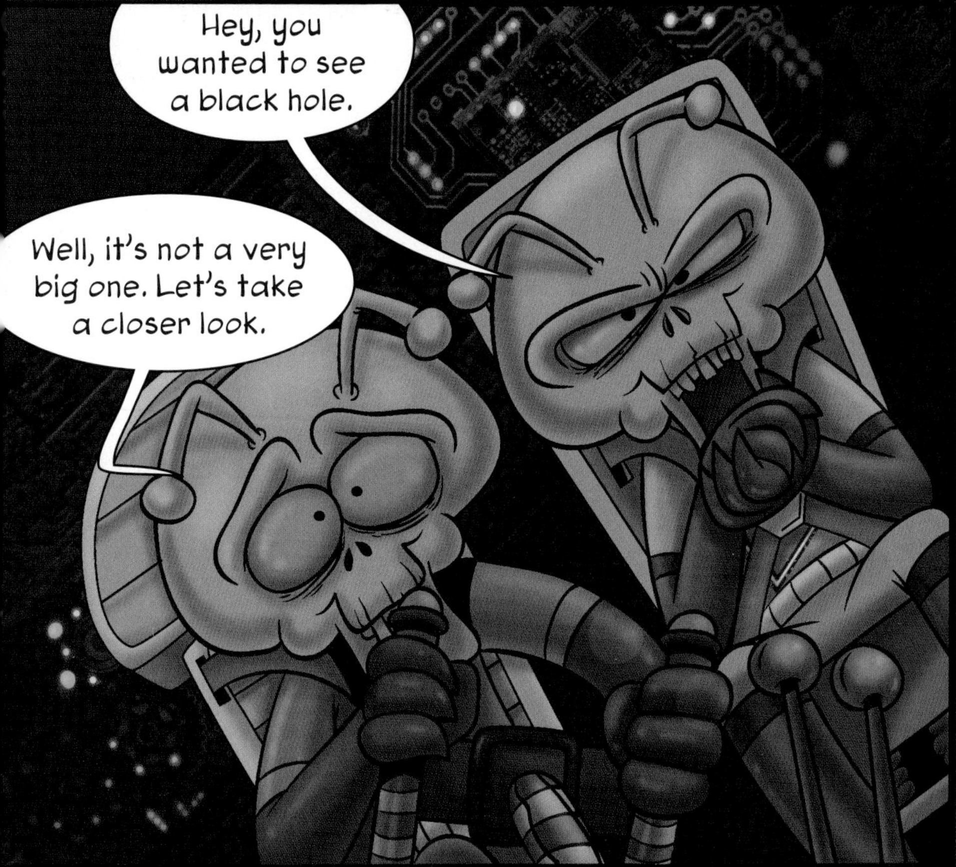
Hey, you wanted to see a black hole.
Well, it's not a very big one. Let's take a closer look.

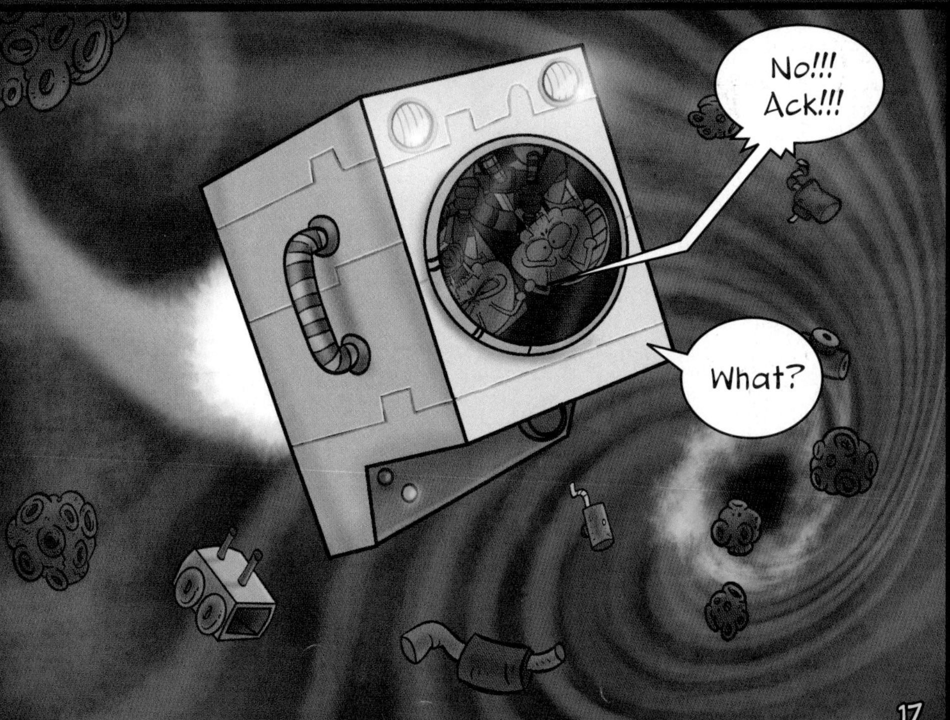
No!!! Ack!!!
What?

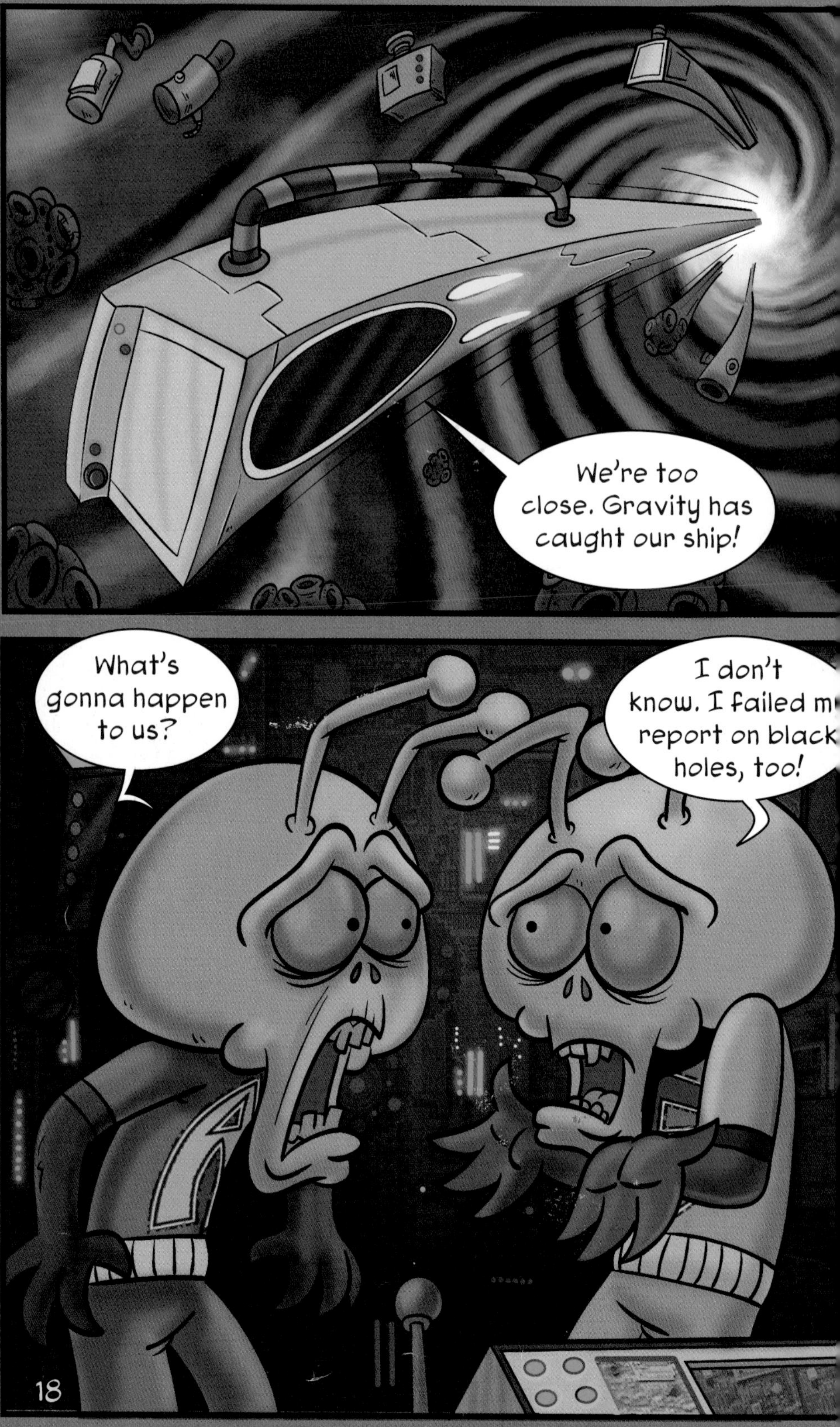
We're too close. Gravity has caught our ship!
What's gonna happen to us?
I don't know. I failed m
report on black
holes, too!

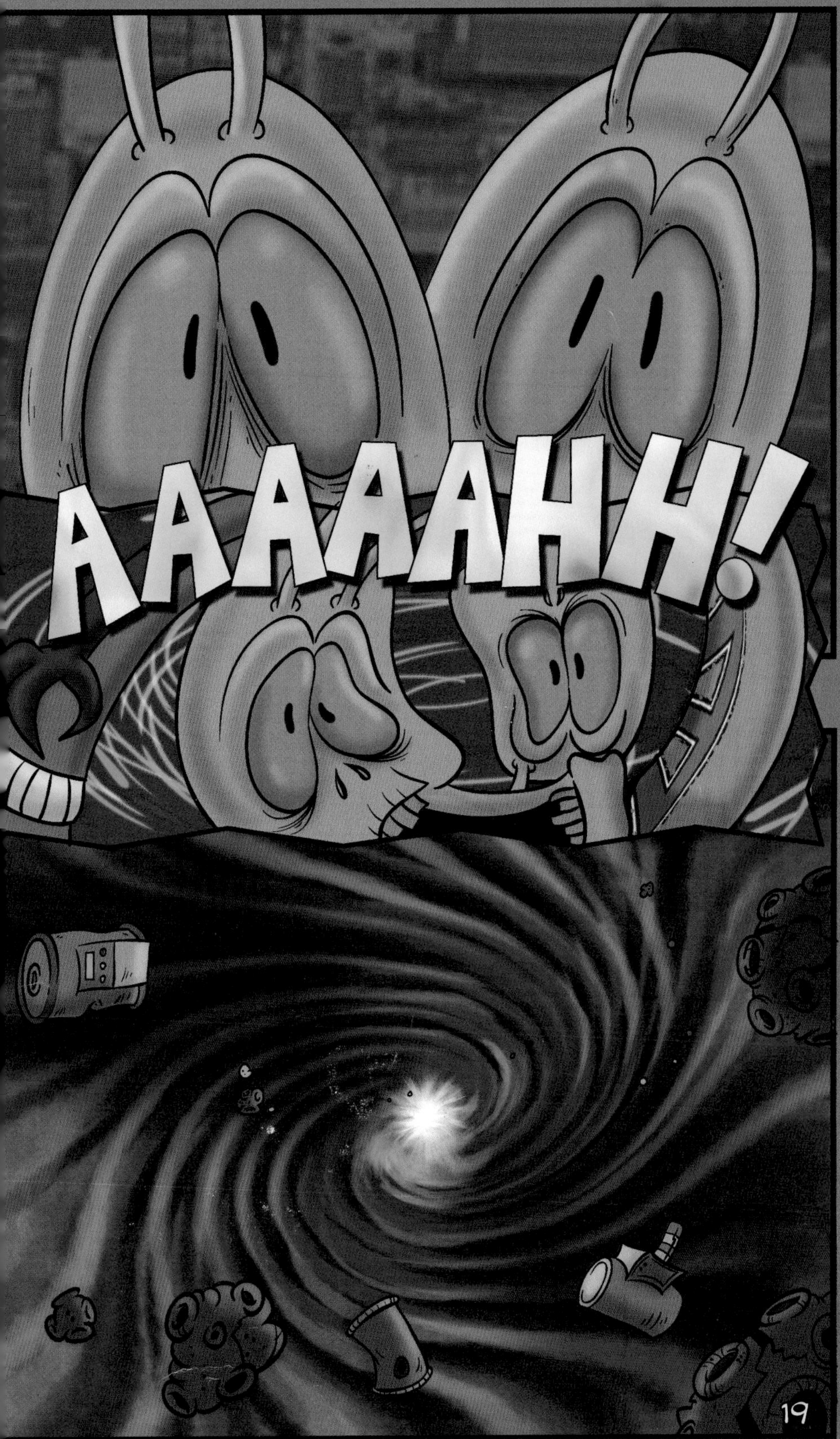
AAAAAHH!

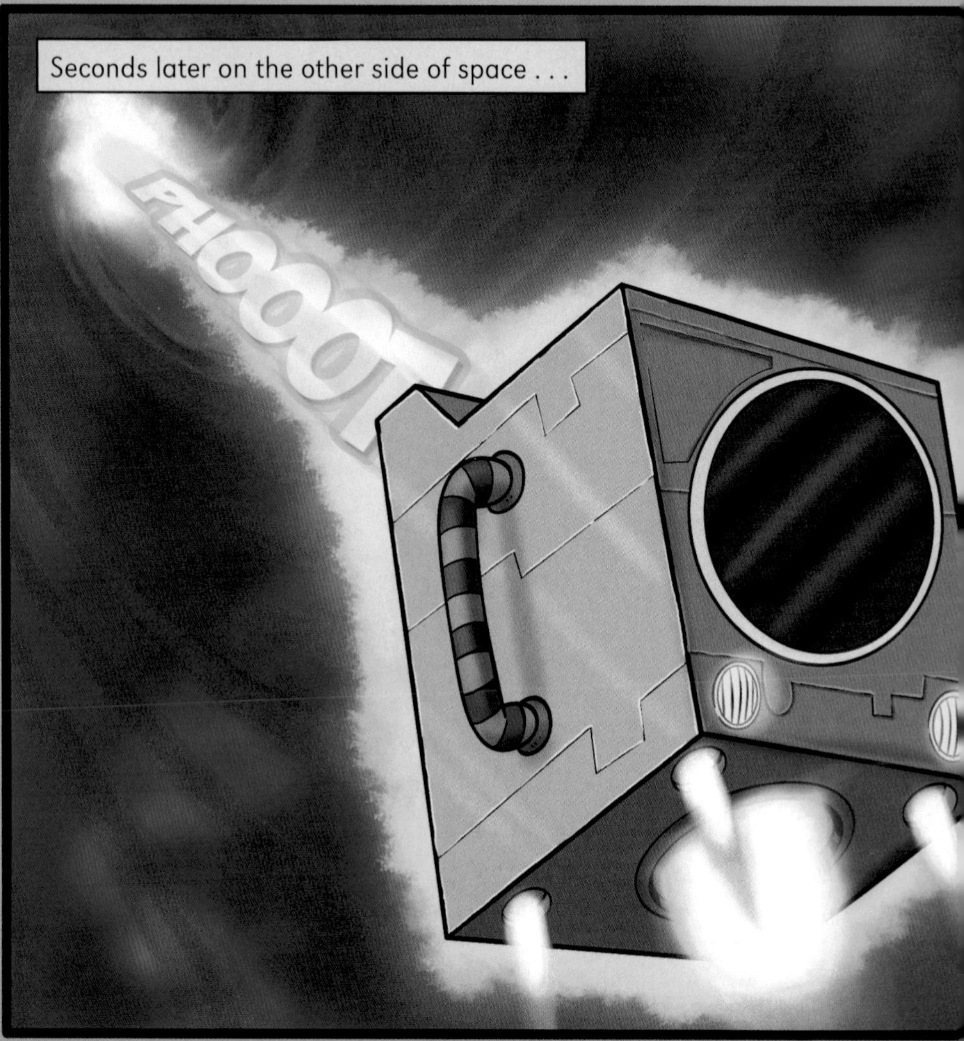
Seconds later on the other side of space . . .
PHOOOT

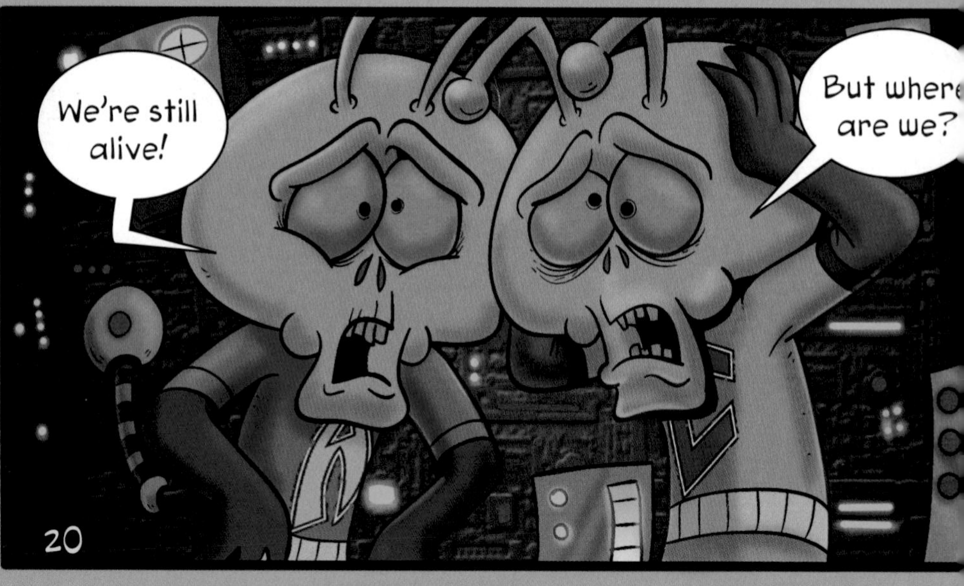
We're still alive!
But where are we?

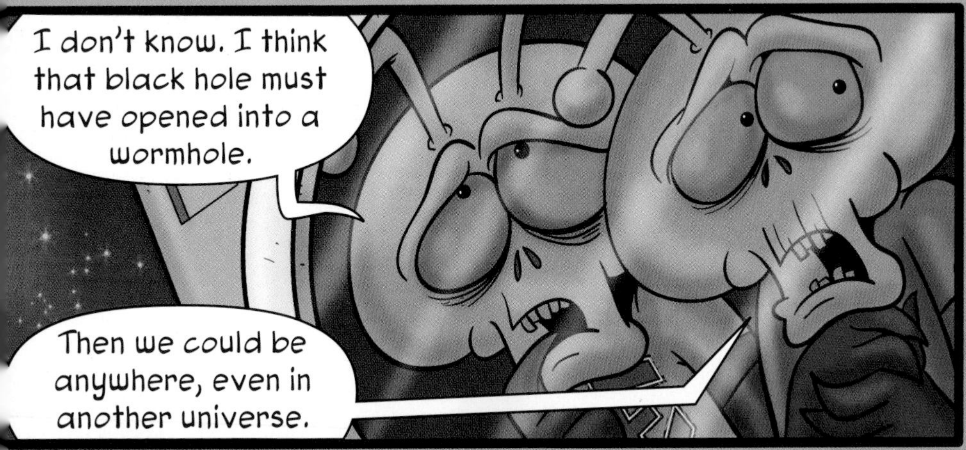
I don't know. I think that black hole must have opened into a wormhole.
Then we could be anywhere, even in another universe.

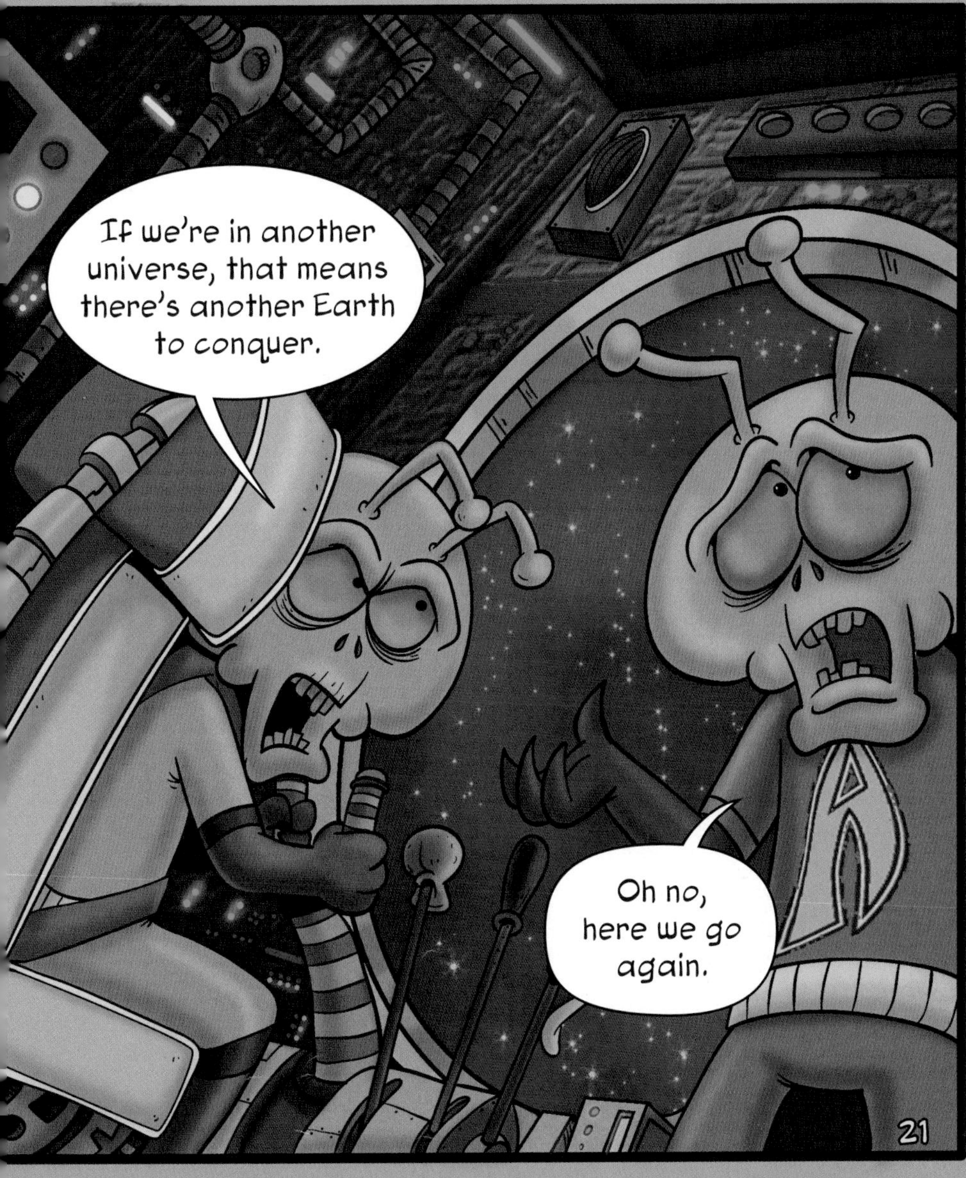
If we're in another universe, that means there's another Earth to conquer.
Oh no, here we go again.

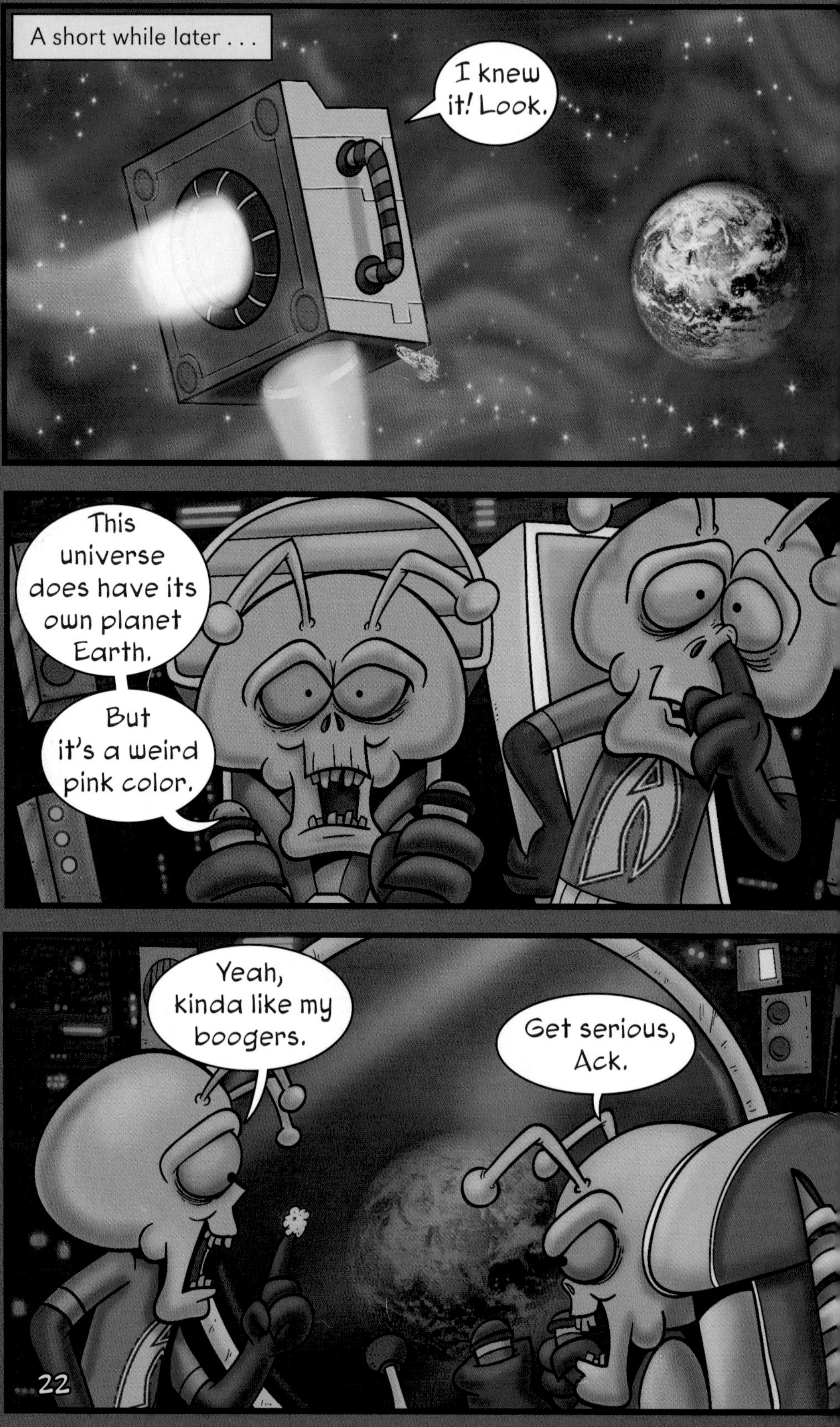

A short while later . . .
I knew it! Look.
This universe does have its own planet Earth.
But it's a weird pink color.
Yeah, kinda like my boogers.
Get serious, Ack.

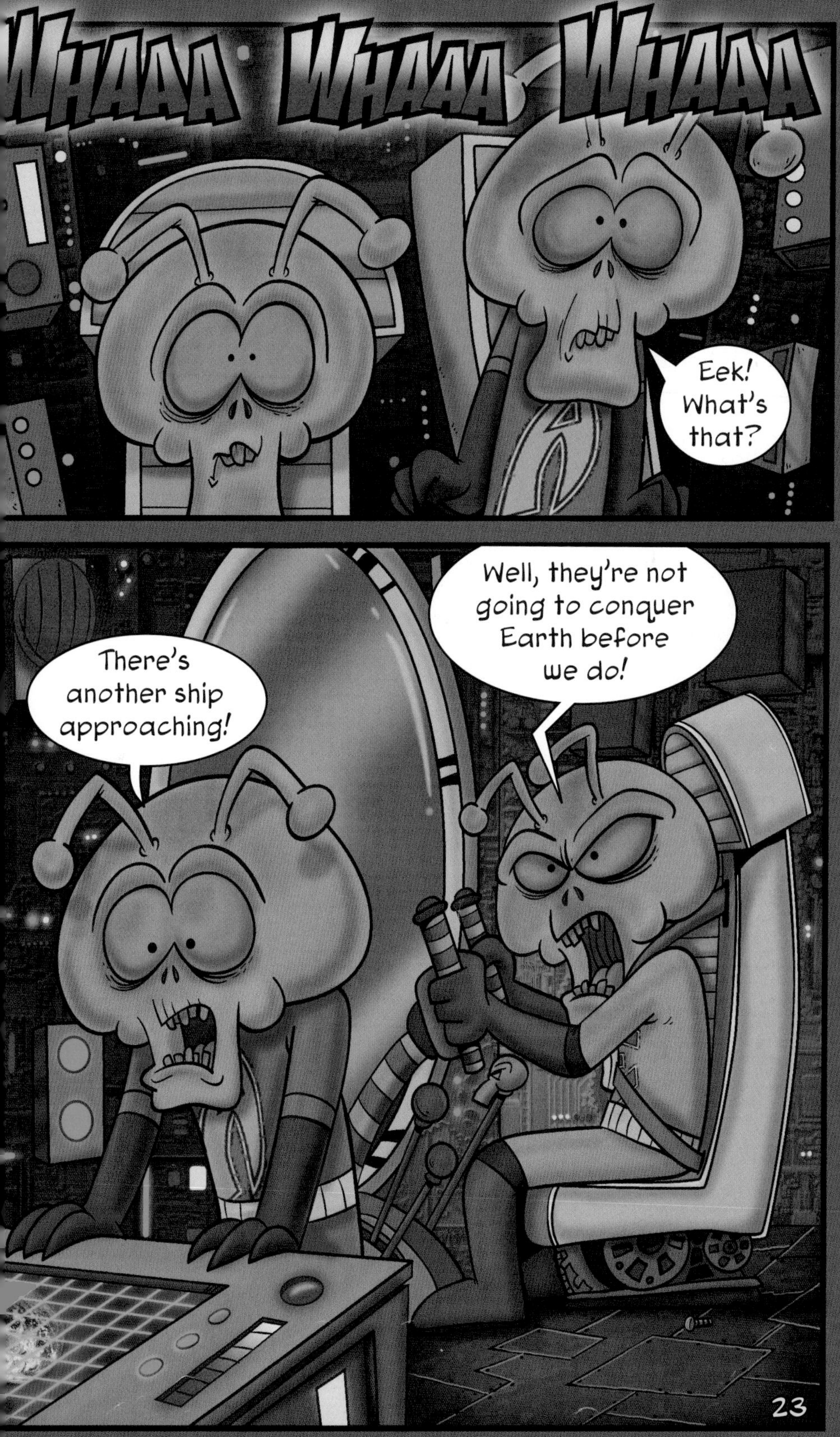
WHAAA WHAAA WHAAA
Eek! What's that?
There's another ship approaching!
Well, they're not going to conquer Earth before we do!

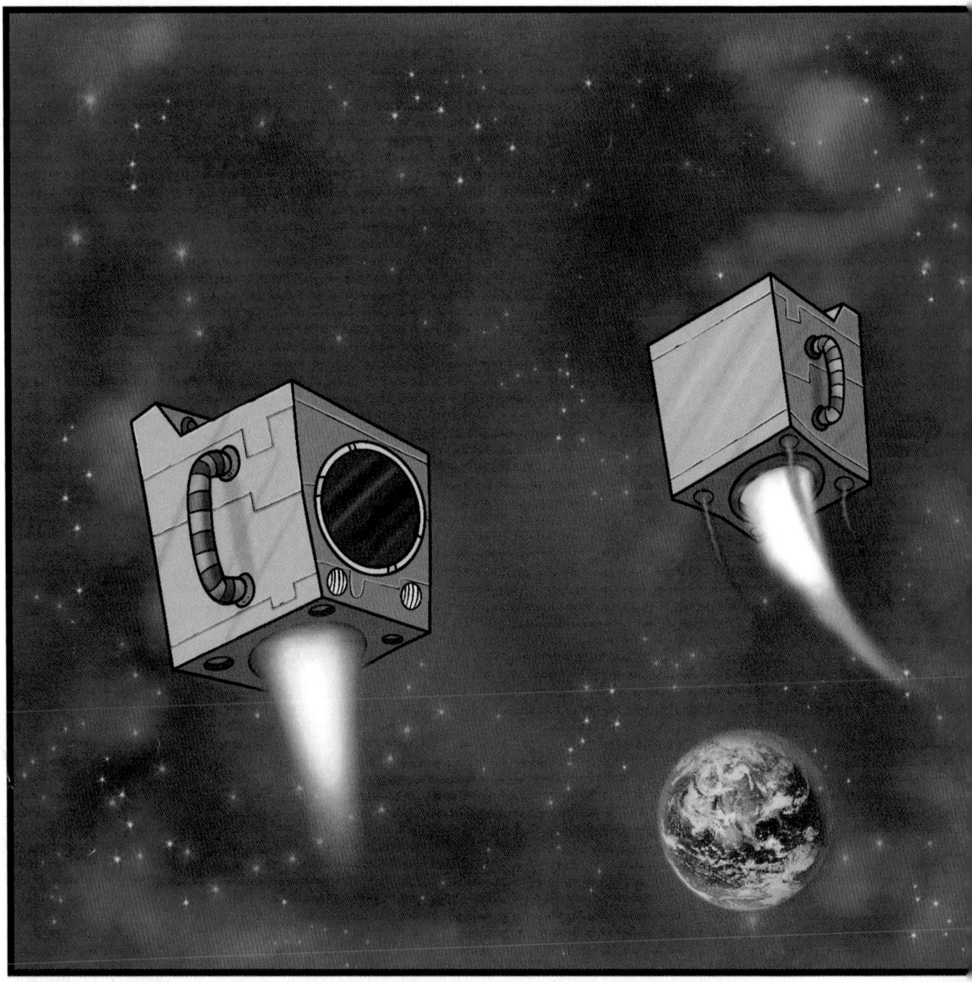

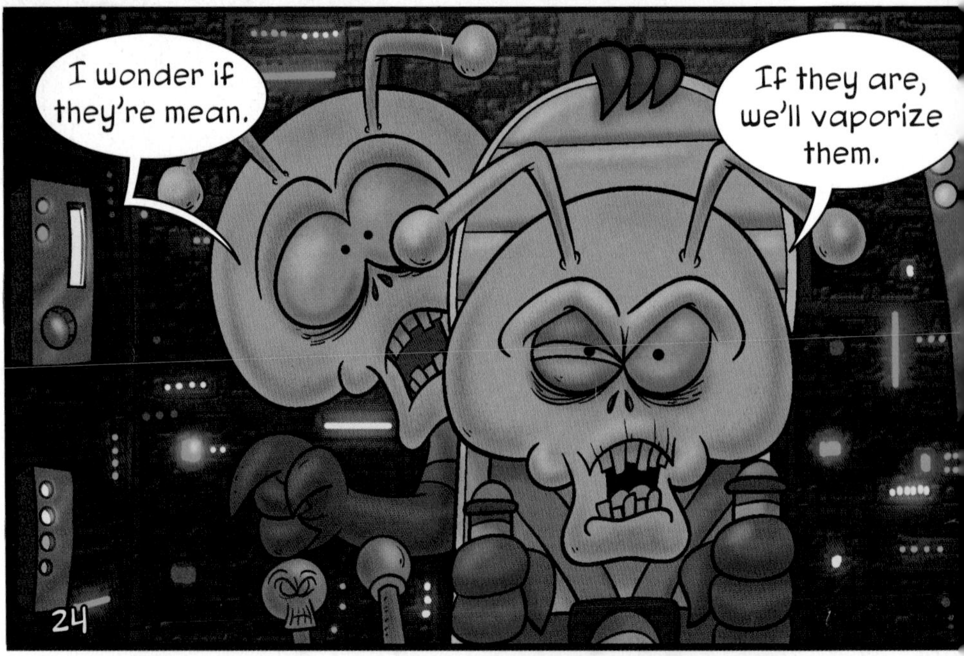
I wonder if they're mean.
If they are, we'll vaporize them.

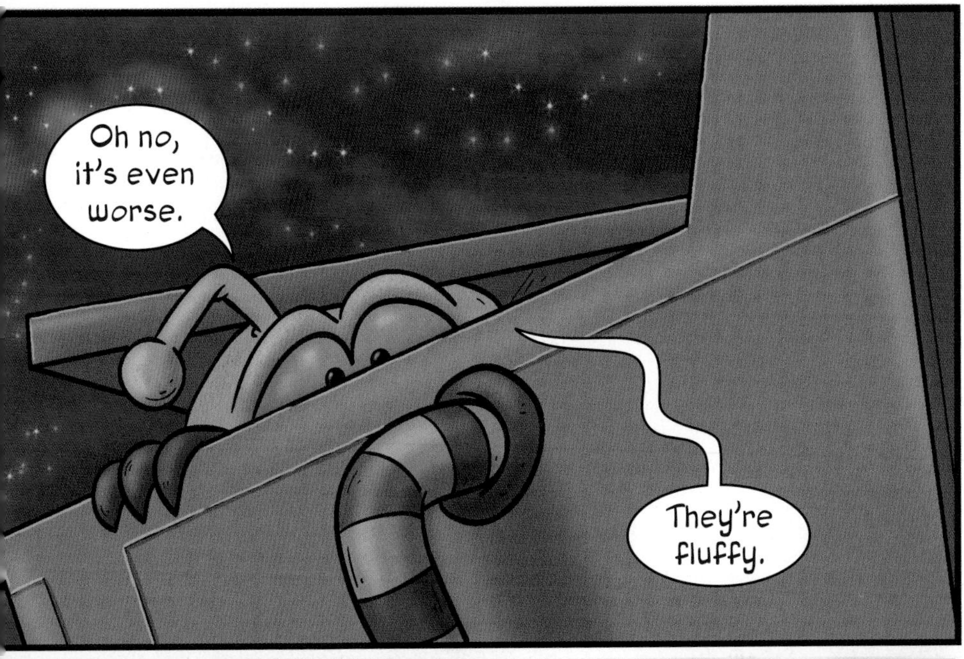
Oh no, it's even worse.
They're fluffy.

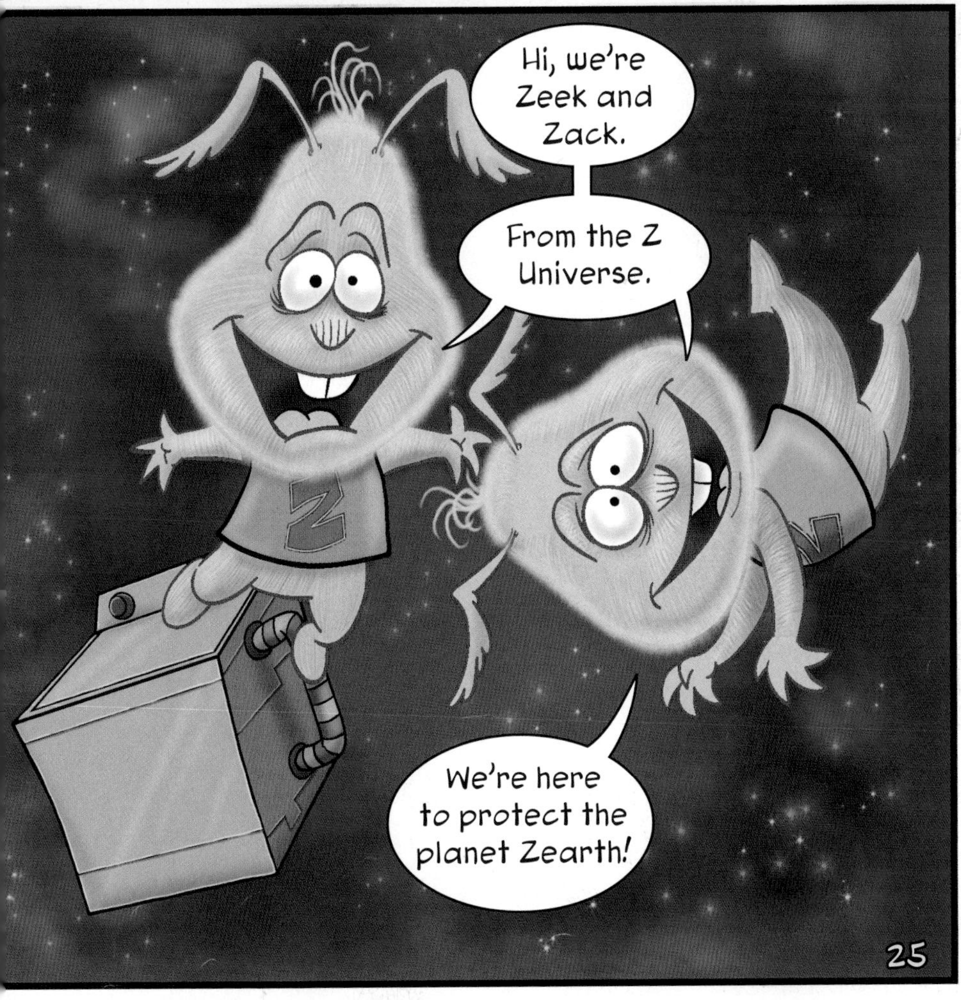
Hi, we're Zeek and Zack.
From the Z Universe.
We're here to protect the planet Zearth!

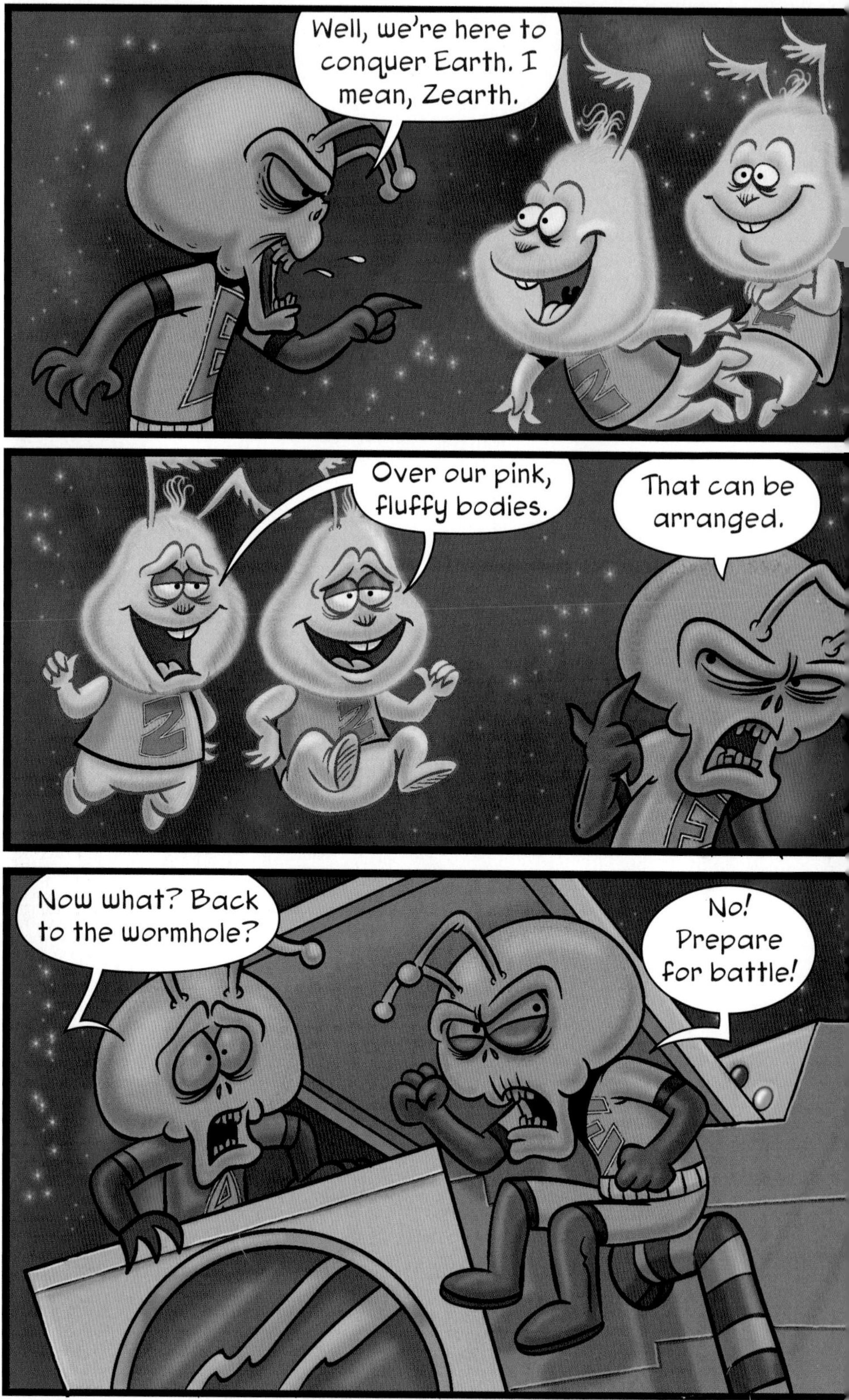
Well, we're here to conquer Earth. I mean, Zearth.
Over our pink, fluffy bodies.
That can be arranged.
Now what? Back to the wormhole?
No! Prepare for battle!

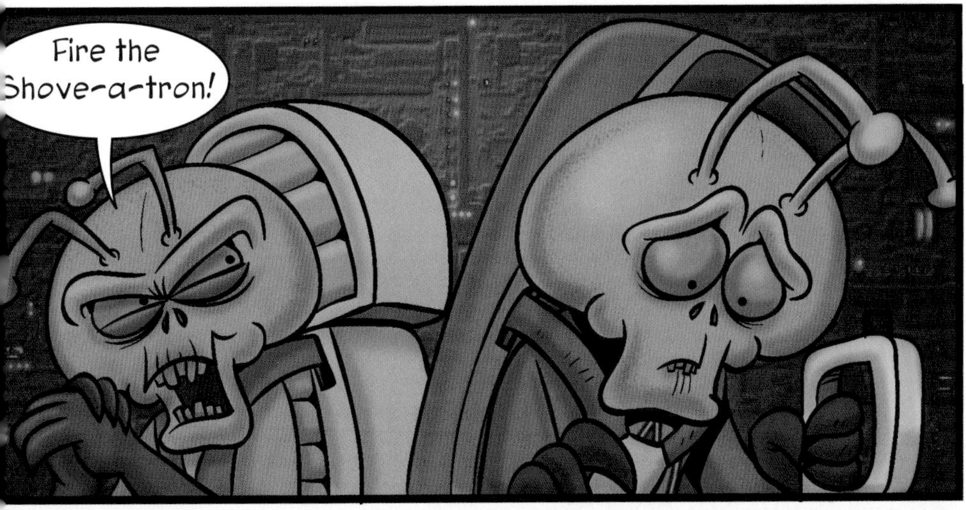
Fire the Shove-a-tron!

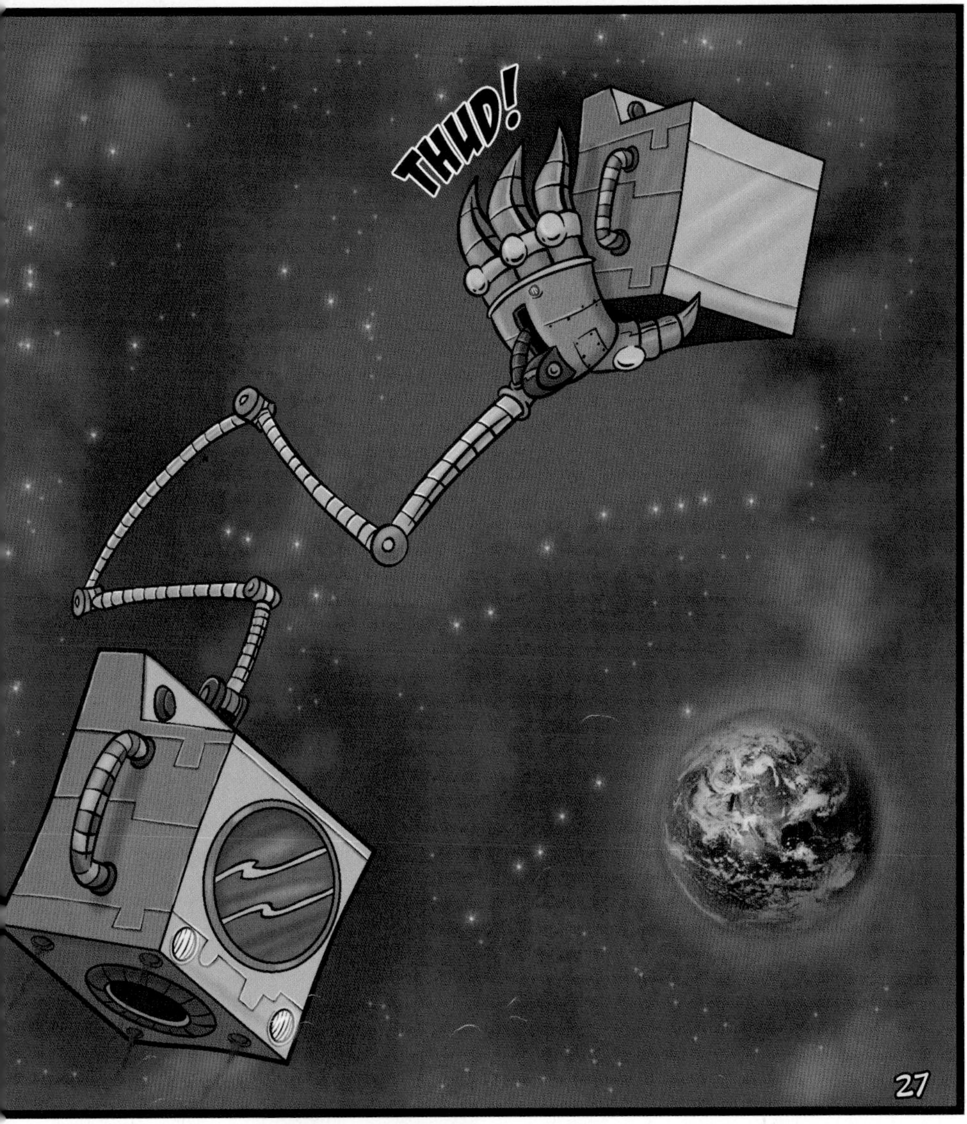
THUD!

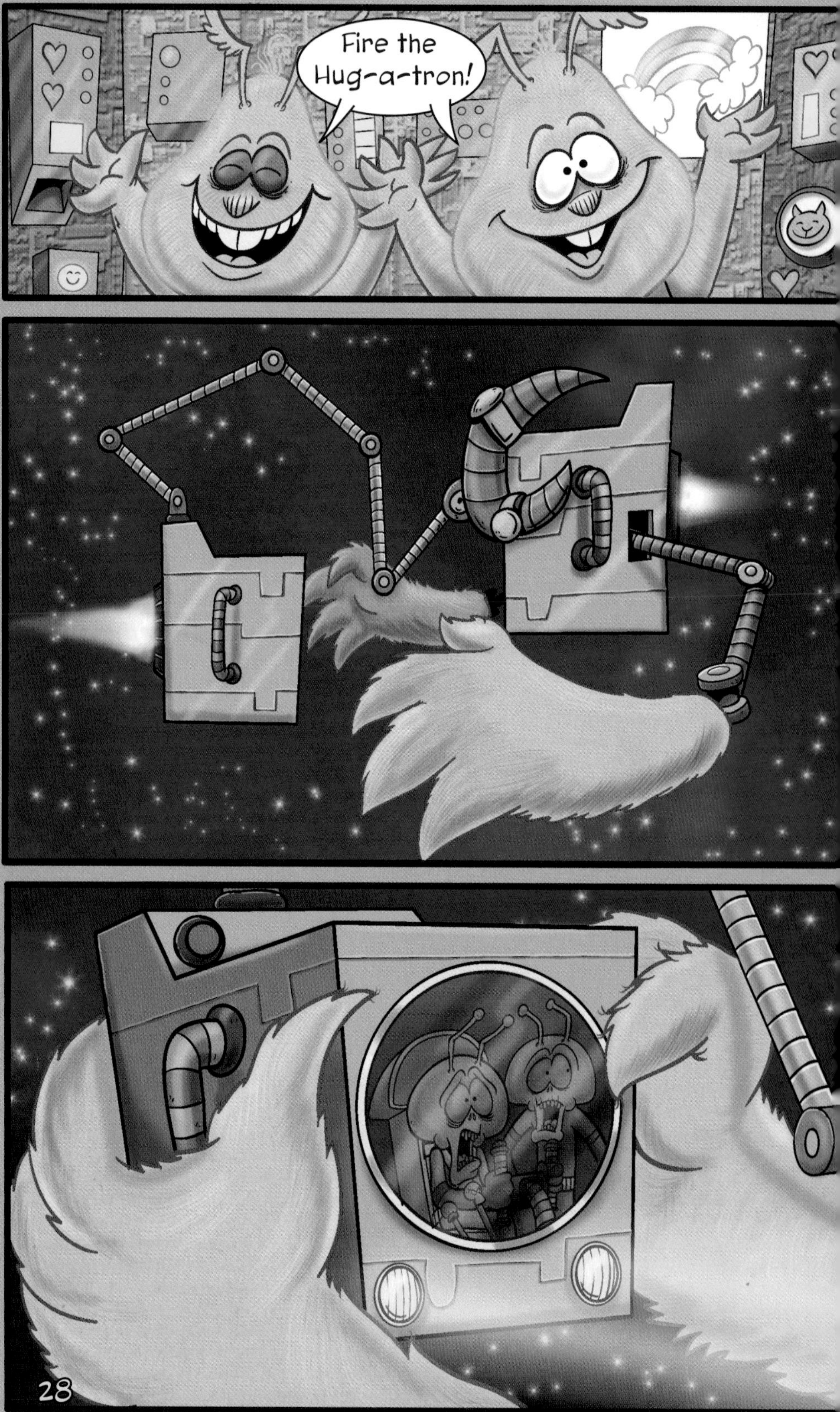
Fire the Hug-a-tron!

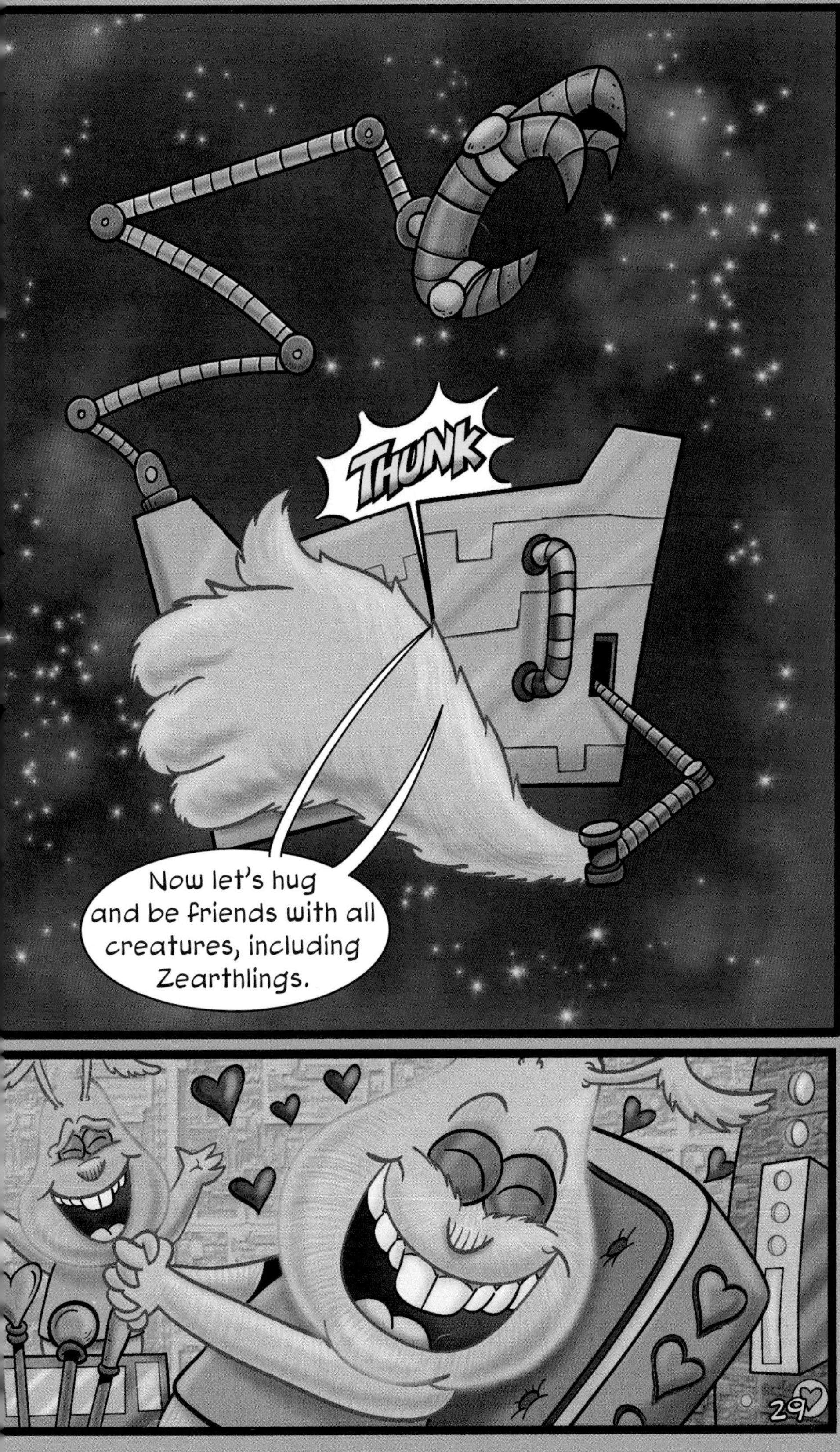
THUNK
Now let's hug and be friends with all creatures, including Zearthlings.

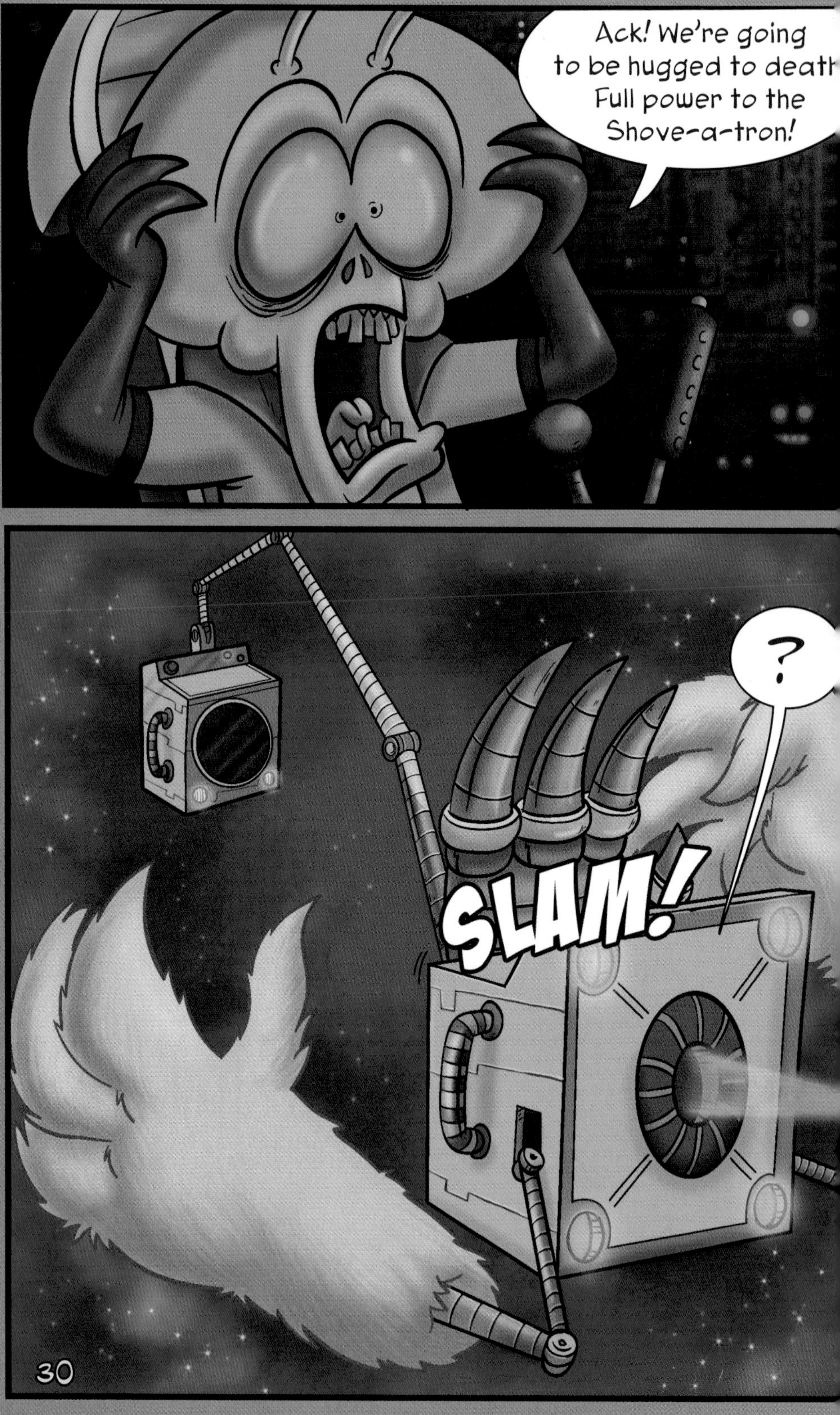
Ack! We're going
to be hugged to deat
Full power to the
Shove-a-tron!
?
SLAM!

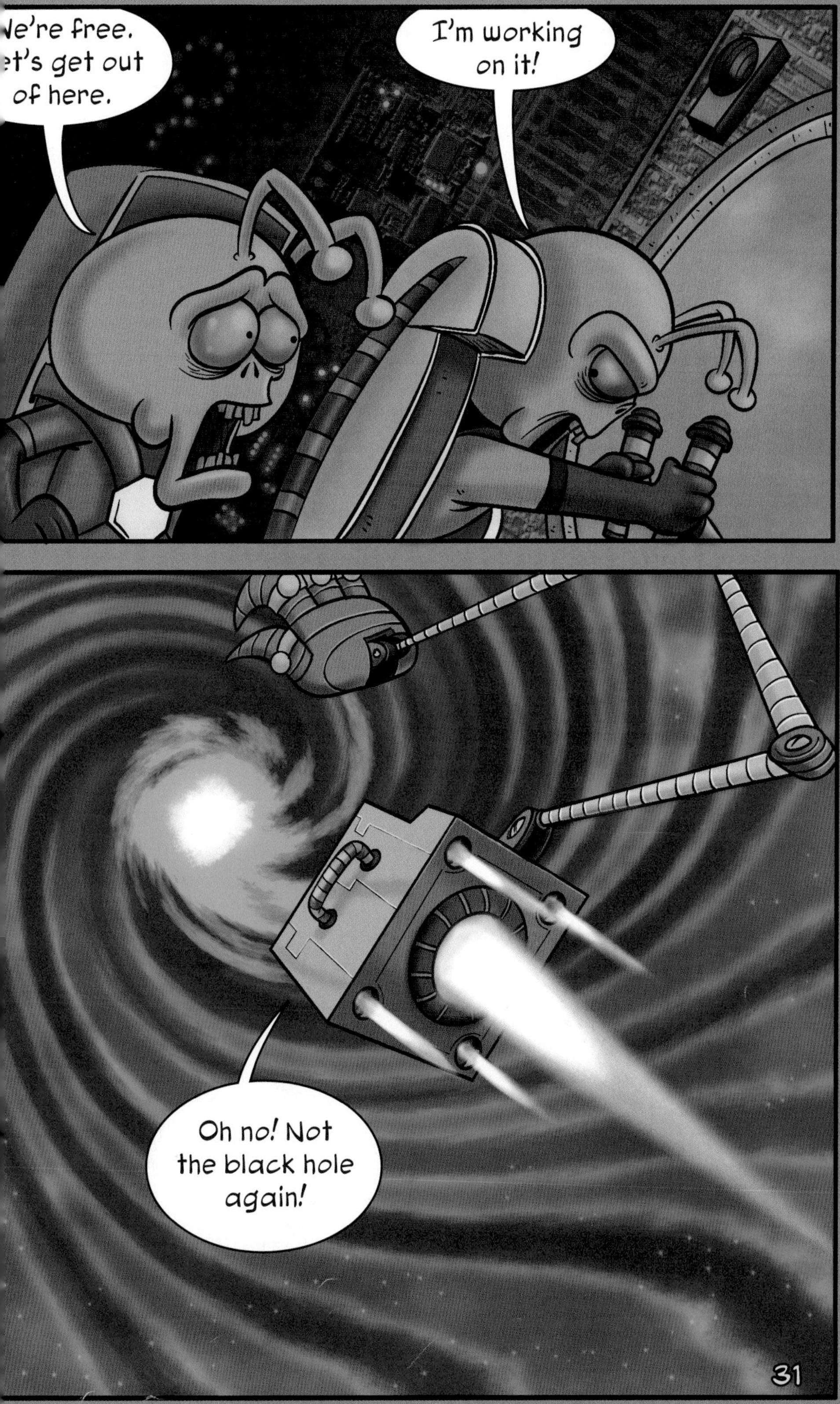
e're free. et's get out of here.
I'm working on it!
Oh no! Not the black hole again!

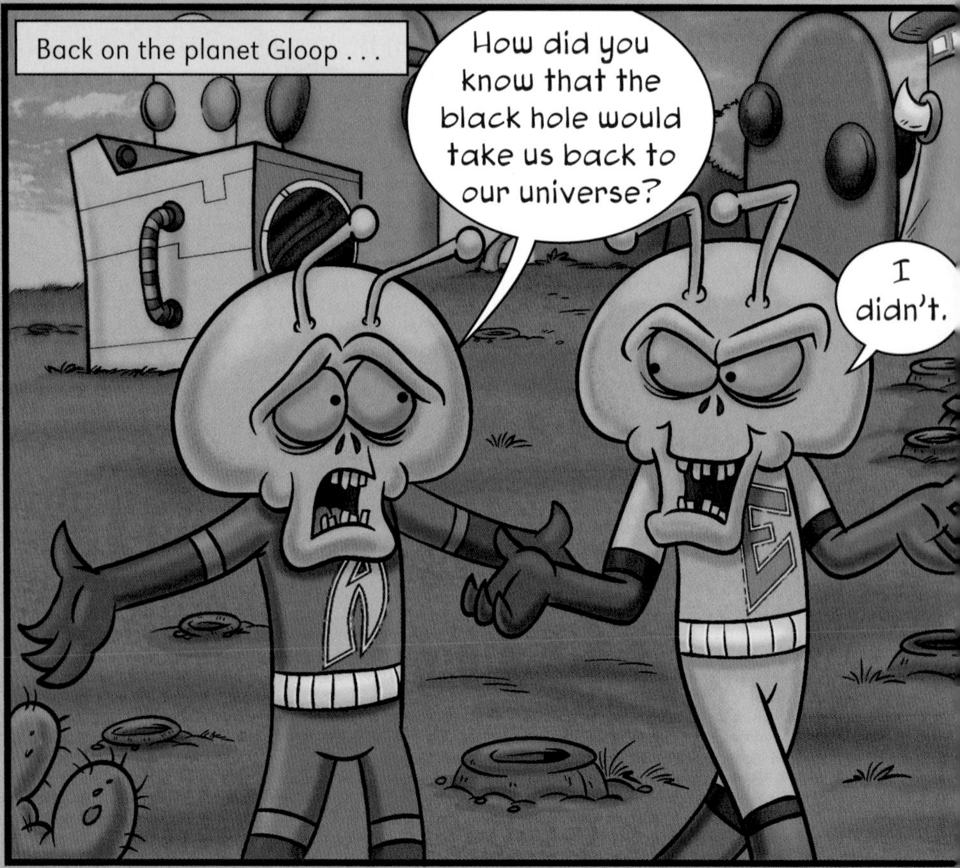
Back on the planet Gloop . . .
How did you know that the black hole would take us back to our universe?
I didn't.

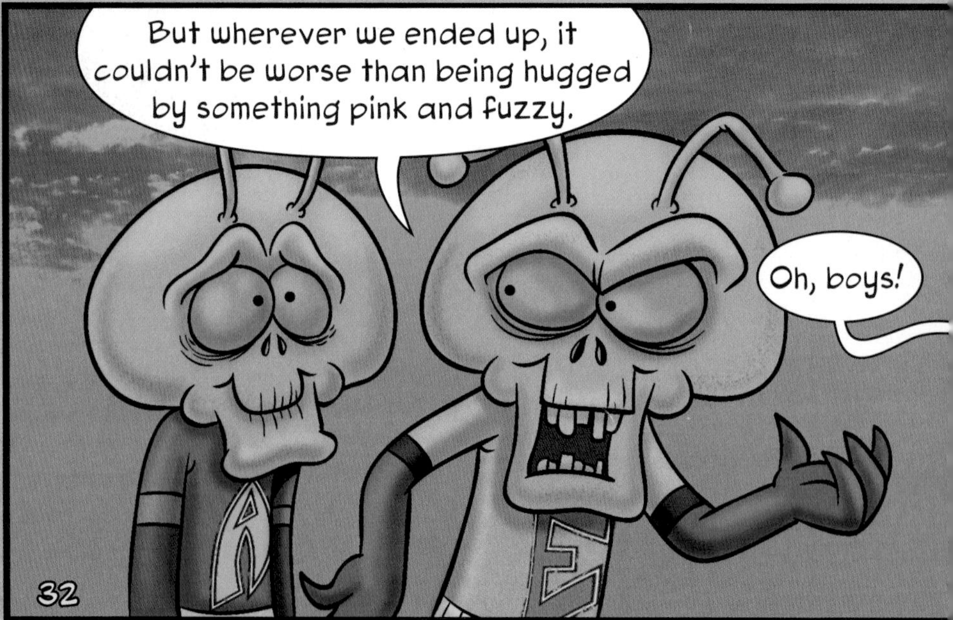
But wherever we ended up, it couldn't be worse than being hugged by something pink and fuzzy.
Oh, boys!

Your Aunt Smooch is joining us for dinner.
Come give your auntie a kiss, boys.
ACK!!!
EEK!!!
THE END

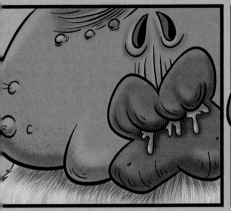

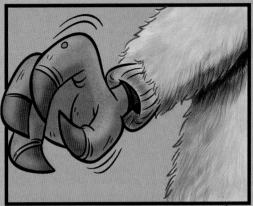

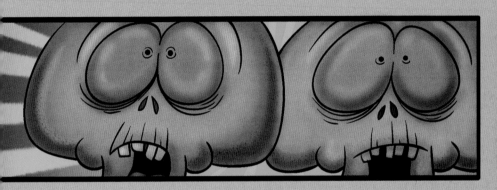

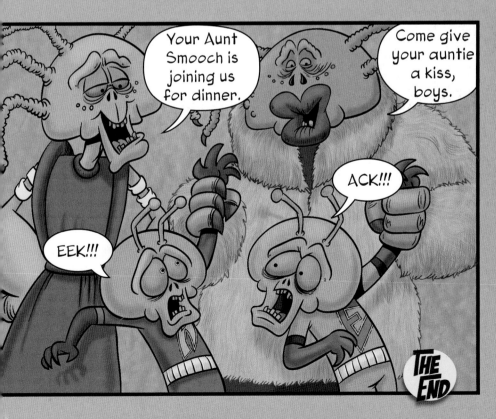

ABOUT THE AUTHOR

Blake A. Hoena once spent a whole weekend just watching his favorite science-fiction movies. Those movies made him wonder what kind of aliens, with their death rays and hyper-drives, couldn't actually conquer Earth. That's when he created Eek and Ack, who play at conquering Earth like earthling kids play at stopping bad guys. Blake has written more than 20 books for children, and currently lives in Minneapolis, Minnesota.

ABOUT THE ILLUSTRATOR

Steve Harpster has loved to draw funny cartoons, mean monsters, and goofy gadgets since he was able to pick up a pencil. In first grade, he avoided writing assignments by working on the pictures for stories instead. Steve was able to land a job drawing funny pictures for books, and that's really what he's best at. Steve lives in Columbus, Ohio, with his wonderful wife, Karen, and their sheepdog, Doodle.

GLOSSARY

black hole (BLAK HOHL)—an object in space with super-strong gravity. Scientists believe black holes are created when stars collapse.

gravity (GRAV-uh-tee)—the powerful force that draws things toward any large object. Stars, planets, and moons all have gravitational pull.

meteoroid (MEE-tee-ur-oyd)—a small space rock that enters a planet or moon's atmosphere

ooze (OOZ)—what aliens do when they go to the bathroom

universe (YOO-nuh-vurs)—everything that is in outer space

vaporize (VAY-puh-ryz)—to turn something into very small pieces, usually done with a ray gun

whizzler drive (WHIZ-luhr DRIVE)—the engine that propels Eek and Ack's ship through space at super speed

wormhole (WURM-hohl)—a tunnel in space that connects two distant places

Z (ZEE)—the worst grade you can receive on the planet Gloop. It's also the last letter in the alphabet and the name for an alternate universe.

Zearth (ZERTH)—a pinkish version of the planet Earth. Zearth is located in the Z universe.

BLACK HOLE FACTS

A black hole is what's left after a massive star dies. The star's intense gravity causes it to collapse into itself, creating a core. The core has such strong gravity that not even light can escape its pull. It is so dense that it sinks into space-time, creating a hole, which is why we call it a black hole. Black holes cannot be seen.

TYPES OF BLACK HOLES

Schwarzchild (SHWARTZ-sheeld)—a black hole that does not have a rotating core

Kerr (KUR)—a black hole with a rotating core. Kerr black holes are the most common. If a star is rotating when it collapses, then a Kerr black hole is created.

THE SIZE OF BLACK HOLES

Our Sun is bigger than 333,000 Earths. Pretty big, right? Black holes are even bigger! Smaller types of black holes, including **micro black holes**, are about the size of our sun. **Supermassive black holes**, however, can have the mass of billions of stars like our sun. Scientists believe that there is a supermassive black hole at the center of most galaxies, including our own, the Milky Way Galaxy.

WORMHOLES AND TIME TRAVEL

No one knows what happens to an object that is sucked into a black hole. Scientist Robert Kerr had a new idea about some rotating black holes. He believed they wouldn't have the crushing gravitational force of most black holes. Kerr thought it might be possible to enter one of these black ones and then exit through a white hole. A **white hole** would be the opposite of a black hole. Instead of sucking objects in, a white hole would spit them out.

The connection between the black and white holes is called a **wormhole**. Wormholes could connect faraway places in space, or even be doors to alternate universes. However, most scientists think that whatever enters a black hole will be crushed and destroyed.

DISCUSSION QUESTIONS

1. Ack receives a Z on his report about black holes. What's the worst grade you've ever received and why? Do you think Ack deserved the grade he received? Explain why you think so.

2. Eek and Ack are brothers, and they look similar, but in what ways are they different? Use examples from the story to explain your answer.

3. Eek and Ack are space aliens from the planet Gloop. Do you believe there are real space aliens? Why or why not?

3. Eek and Ack are disgusted by all things pink and fuzzy. Is there something that disgusts you? Describe what you find disgusting about it.

2. Eek is constantly thinking up sinister plots to conquer Earth. If you were Eek, how would you conquer our big, blue home? Write it down!

1. If you flew through a wormhole and ended up in a different universe with another Earth, what would it be like? How would the plants and animals be different from what we have here on our Earth?

WRITING PROMPTS

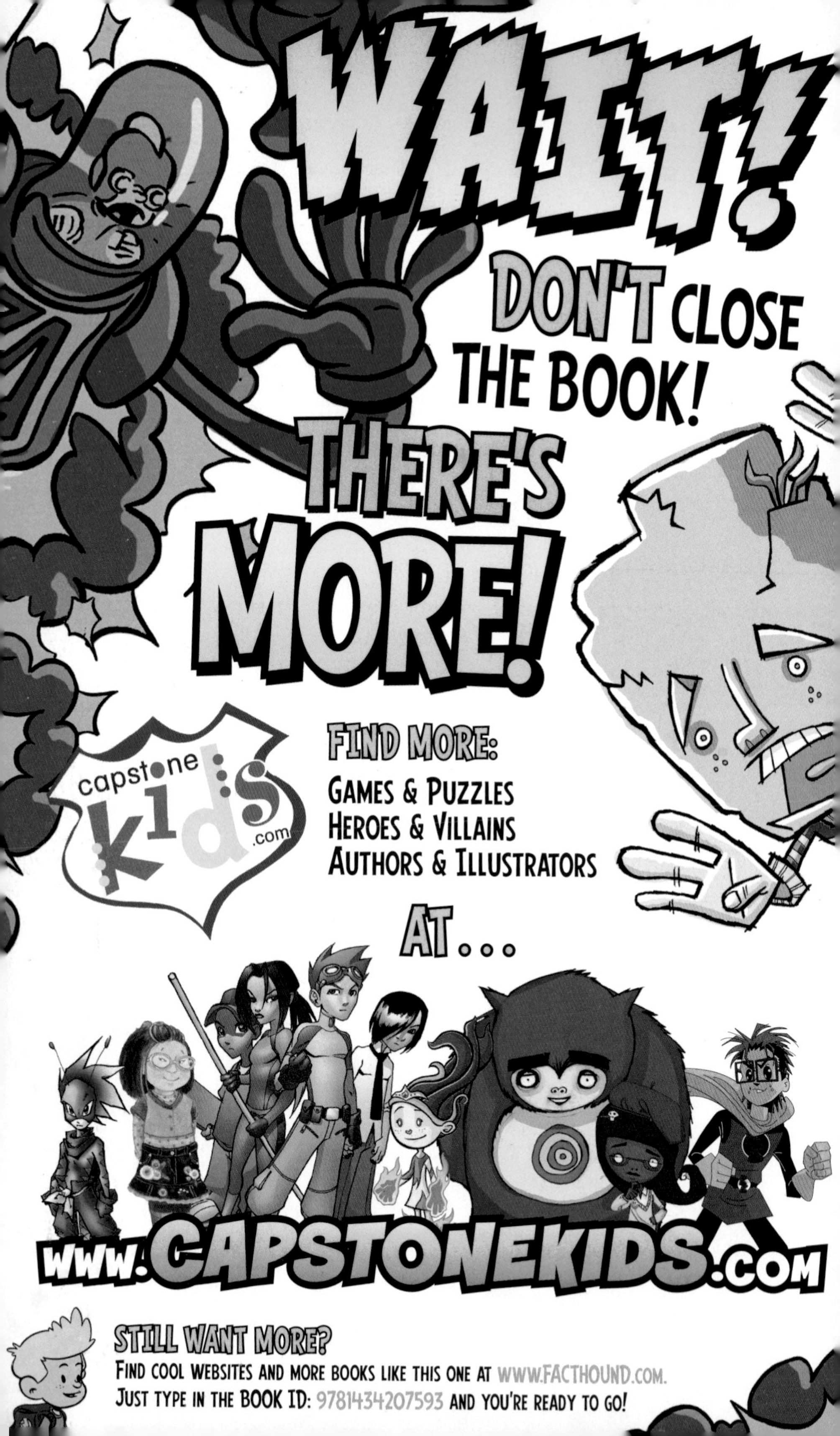
WAIT!
DON'T CLOSE THE BOOK!
THERE'S MORE!
capstone kids .com
FIND MORE:
GAMES & PUZZLES
HEROES & VILLAINS
AUTHORS & ILLUSTRATORS
AT...
WWW.CAPSTONEKIDS.COM
STILL WANT MORE?
FIND COOL WEBSITES AND MORE BOOKS LIKE THIS ONE AT WWW.FACTHOUND.COM.
JUST TYPE IN THE BOOK ID: 9781434207593 AND YOU'RE READY TO GO!